Blast For Me

Lock Down Publications and Ca$h Presents

Blast For Me

A Novel by *Ghost*

Blast For Me

Lock Down Publications
P.O. Box 870494
Mesquite, Tx 75187

Copyright 2017 by Blast For Me by Ghost

All rights reserved. No part of this book may be reproduced in any form or by electronic or mechanical means, including information storage and retrieval systems without permission in writing from the publisher, except by a reviewer who may quote brief passages in review.
First Edition December 2017
Printed in the United States of America

This is a work of fiction. Names, characters, places, and incidents either are products of the author's imagination or are used fictitiously. Any similarity to actual events or locales or persons, living or dead, is entirely coincidental.

Lock Down Publications
Like our page on Facebook: Lock Down Publications @
www.facebook.com/lockdownpublications.ldp
Cover design and layout by: **Dynasty Cover Me**
Book interior design by: **Shawn Walker**
Edited by: **Kiera Northington**

Ghost

Stay Connected with Us!

Text **LOCKDOWN** to 22828 to stay up-to-date
with new releases, sneak peaks, contests and more…
Or CLICK HERE to sign up.

Thank you!

Like our page on Facebook:

Lock Down Publications: Facebook

Join Lock Down Publications/The New Era
Reading Group

Follow us on Instagram:

Lock Down Publications: Instagram

Email Us**:** We want to hear from you!

Submission Guideline.

Submit the first three chapters of your completed manuscript to ldpsubmissions@gmail.com, subject line: Your book's title. The manuscript must be in a .doc file and sent as an attachment. Document should be in Times New Roman, double spaced and in size 12 font. Also, provide your synopsis and full contact information. If sending multiple submissions, they must each be in a separate email.

Have a story but no way to send it electronically? You can still submit to LDP/Ca$h Presents. Send in the first three chapters, written or typed, of your completed manuscript to:

LDP: Submissions Dept
Po Box 870494
Mesquite, Tx 75187

DO NOT send original manuscript. Must be a duplicate.

Provide your synopsis and a cover letter containing your full contact information.

Thanks for considering LDP and Ca$h Presents.

Dedications

This book is dedicated to my precious baby girl 3/10. I love you more than anything and everything in this world. You're the reason why I'm putting the birds down and trying to find another way. You deserve the best possible future.

Acknowledgements

Mad love to all of The LDP family. We got this!

Lil' Momma and Jennifer, two of the strongest women
I've had the pleasure of getting to know.

Thank you for entrusting me with y'all deepest darkest
most precious secrets. I hope I did y'all stories some
justice with what I have produced. It takes a lot of
courage to pick up the pieces of y'all lives after what's
been thrown. You ladies are magnificent. Continue to be
strong and live without fear. God bless.

There's no greater blessing to the world than the black
woman.

Ghost

Blast For Me

Chapter 1
Lil' Momma

"You always said you wanted to see what I do, here's your front row seat. Huh, pull this down over yo face. If somethin' go wrong, I don't want niggaz knowin' it was you I had wit me. You make sure you stay back a lil' bit and just watch how daddy get down," J.T. instructed, handing me an all-black mask.

I could feel my heart beat; every single thump pounding into my chest. Grabbing the mask, I smoothed it over my face, hands trembling with fear. We were at this guy named Red's house, preparing ourselves in his bathroom, our eyes peering out the window, as we saw him pull into the driveway.

Red's baby mother, Molly, had let us in informing us that Red had stepped out, but was supposed to have been back over an hour ago. I had never met Molly before that day. J.T. had introduced me as his cousin from out of town, and after we smoked a few blunts with her, she decided to throw a pizza into the oven, and that's when J.T. asked her if I could use the bathroom.

Once she gave the okay, he offered to show me where it was. I didn't know what he had in mind, but I knew before it was all said and done, there would be plenty of bloodshed.

From the bathroom's window, we could see the curb and that's when I saw Red's cocaine white Lexus pulling up to the curb, beating the sounds of Kendrick Lamar.

J.T frowned. "I'm finna fuck this nigga over in a major way. I like when mafuckas think it's sweet." He reached over, adjusting the mask on my face. "Baby, the only reason I got you wit me this time is 'cuz I trust you. You always thinkin' I'm out here on some bullshit, when all I'm doin' is makin' sure we keep eatin' by any means. This is how daddy provides."

He went into his waistband and pulled out two chrome pistols, cocking first one and then the other. "Remember to stay back a lil' bit, but don't miss nothin'. I wanna break you in the right way and show you what this ski mask shit all about. It's the only way you gon' learn."

I stood there shaking like a leaf on a tree when the wind blows. I was scared out of my mind. I wanted to ask him so many questions, but I couldn't get my brain to form the questions, and even if I did, my tongue would have been too scared to relay them.

Out of the window, we watched Red get out of the car. He had a big blunt in his mouth, carrying a bottle of Hennessy in his other hand, walking towards the house. I could make out his liquor of choice, being that it was all me and J.T. drank together. He paused in his tracks taking the blunt from his mouth, looked to the sky, shielding his eyes from the sun. Putting the blunt back to his lips, he took a pull from it, and continued his stride toward the house. Even from the bathroom, we could hear his heavy footsteps on the porch.

Red was a big man. He had to be about two hundred and eighty pounds. Light-skinned, with long cornrows he kept braided straight to the back. J.T. and I had gone to Crenshaw High School with him, but J.T. knew him longer, being that they had grown up together, but I had only known Red since the tenth grade.

He was a major player when it came to the women. He played on the football team, at the same time, selling weed and pills. So, his name was ringing. I didn't know the complete history between him and J.T., but I had assumed for the most part, they were really cool.

J.T. cradled my head in his hands and planted a soft kiss onto my lips, snatching me from my thoughts. "You betta still love me afterwards, too." He laughed as he pulled open the bathroom door, just as Red walked past it.

Something must've made Red look in the direction of the opening door, and as soon as he did, *Bam!*

J.T. slammed the handle of the gun into Red's forehead. "Bitch ass nigga, you thought it was sweet!" J.T. roared, as Red fell backward, holding his face.

Before he had the chance to process what was going on, J.T. straddled him, and smacked him across the face with the pistol again. *Wham!* Knocking him out cold, his face covered in blood.

Molly stood about twenty feet away in the living room, both hands covering her mouth, in a state of shock. "Holy shit! Look J.T., I don't know what he done did to you, but please don't take it out on me. I ain't got nothing to do with it." She turned around and looked like she was getting ready to try and make a dash to back door, but J.T. was on her ass.

Before she could even make it into the kitchen where the door was located, J.T. grabbed her by her long micro braids and yanked her to the floor. She fell with a loud boom! "Bitch, I ain't one of them niggas that won't kill a woman. I don't give a fuck, you been spendin' my money wit this nigga. Now, you finna tell where the rest of my shit at."

Whap! He slapped her across the face so hard, it sounded like somebody had gotten smacked on their naked back.

"Ahhhhh," she screamed.

"Where my shit at?"

"Okay, J.T., damn! Calm down! I'll take you to it," she said, with blood spilling out of her mouth, looking like she had gargled a bunch of tomato paste and left her mouth open for it to spill out. I could see her lips were already swelling up.

J.T. pulled her up by her hair roughly. "Let's go then, bitch. I ain't got time to be playin' these games with you, or that nigga. Ain't neither one of you mafuckas innocent in my eyes." He pushed her roughly in front of him. "Where's it at?"

She fell to the floor on her yellow knees. She was a small woman, like me. She couldn't have weighed more than one hundred and twenty pounds. She also looked mixed, but I couldn't tell with what right off the bat. "I'mma show you." She started to crawl into the kitchen. He yanked her back up by her hair, and she screamed.

"J.T.! Why are you doing me like this? Me and you ain't never had no problems before." Tears sailed down her cheeks, with her lips as big as boxing gloves.

He took one of the guns and put it to her forehead. "Bitch, I'mma tell you one more time to take me to my money. If I have to tell you again, I'mma blow yo shit all over this floor and find it myself. Now, where is it?" he hollered.

She jumped up and pointed to the deep freezer in their kitchen. "It's in the bottom of there, wrapped up in a black plastic garbage bag. Just take it and leave. Please, J.T., we don't want no more trouble," she whined, blood dripping from her lips.

He stepped to the side of her and threw open the top of the freezer. Looking at me, he instructed, "Throw all that shit out, until you see a black plastic bag this bitch says is in there." Looking at her, he warned, "If it ain't, I'm splashin' you all over this kitchen."

"It is though. Please let me go when you get it. I gotta take care of my son, J.T. Please don't take me away from him," she begged, dropping to her knees with her fingers interlocked.

Following his directives, I got to tossing out the freezer's contents so fast, not caring where they landed. My main focus was getting the money, and getting the fuck out of there before

J.T. killed somebody. That was the last thing I wanted him to do.

He had a horrible temper. It never was toward me, but I saw him get down a few times in the streets, and I knew he was a force to be reckoned with when upset.

After throwing out enough stuff, I finally came upon the black plastic bag all the way at the bottom of the freezer. I was so happy, I couldn't help but smile. "I see it, baby," I said, pulling at it. For some reason, it didn't come up. It was stuck.

J.T. looked into the freezer, and a big smile crept across his face. He leaned in, yanking the big bag out with one try, damn near knocking over the whole freezer in the process. He threw the bag on the floor right by the stove.

"Open that mafucka and tell me what's in it."

I dropped down to my knees and started ripping into it. The bag was cool to the touch. I took my fingers and poked a hole in the plastic, before ripping it open like a madman.

As soon as I saw the bundles of money, my eyes got as big as Ferris Wheels. "It's all money, daddy, now what?"

He smiled, "Yeah, that's what I'm talkin' about."

"Can you please let me go now J.T.? I did my part," Molly pleaded.

J.T. reached down and picked her up by the neck, lifting her into the air. "You think this shit over, after you and that nigga crossed me and been spendin' my money!" He let her down some and then wrapped his arm around her neck from behind, dragging her into the living room where Red was shaking his head, trying to come out of his slumber.

As soon as J.T. got her into the living room, he threw her down to the floor right next to Red. She landed on top of him and must have kneed him in the nuts, because he threw her off him immediately, with his hands between his legs, cupping his jewels. "Fuck! Man, why you doin' this shit, J.T.? I thought we was niggas!"

As he talked, blood poured from his mouth in large globs. He had a small hole on his forehead that also had blood leaking out of it. It pooled onto his face, and dripped down the sides of his neck.

J.T. knelt beside him, and placed his hand around the back of Red's neck, pulling him upward until his bleeding forehead was against the barrel of his gun. "Bitch nigga, you kept more of the money than you should have. I put you up on that fuckin' lick. That nigga said he got hit for a hundred G's. How the fuck you 'n dis bitch sayin' it was only twenty-five!" He slapped him across the face with the pistol. *Wham!* "Bitch nigga!"

Red spit out a tooth that flew into the wall and wound up on the carpet by my foot. It looked like a fang, with blood at the root of it. All I could do was swallow my nervousness. *We gotta get the fuck outta here.*

Red coughed up a glob of blood that pooled over his bottom lip. "It wasn't no hundred G's, nigga. That fool lyin'. It was only twenty-five, just like we told you. That nigga just puttin' a hunnit on ten, that's it." He tried to sit up, but to no avail.

Wham! J.T. striked him across the face again, hitting him in the mouth, causing him to spit out more than a few teeth all over the carpet.

"J.T., you got yo money now. How about you just let us skate on this one? I mean what more do you have to prove? Plus, my son gon' be home soon. I don't want him to walk in on this shit. This would destroy his innocence," Molly said.

J.T. looked at her and smiled. "I'mma tell you the truth, Molly, this nigga here finna die one way or the other. The only

14

thing I'm tryna decide is if I'm gon' kill you, too. You know how shit goes in L.A., ain't no such thing as leavin' a witness."

She dropped to her knees and started wailing at the top of her lungs. "J.T., please don't kill me. I'm begging you! I'll do anything. Please!" She clasped her fingers together and shook them in the air. "I'm only twenty-three years old. I'm way too young to die."

While she was thinking she was too young to die, I was thinking I was too young to be charged with murder. I was only twenty-four years old. In fact, I had just turned twenty-four two weeks ago. I was getting more and more afraid as to what was about to happen.

J.T. got up and threw her on top of Red. "I'll tell you what. You said you'd do anything, right? That's what you said, am I right?"

She looked up to him nervously. "I will, but can't you just let us go?"

He laughed. "Oh hell, nawl. We gon' do this shit one way. Now, I told you this nigga about to die no matter what, it's death because of dishonor. That's how we get down in Compton. And yo nigga know that. So, we gon' do this shit like this. Either you about to kill this nigga the way I want you to, or I'm gon' kill him and you. Then, when yo son gets home, I'mma body his ass fresh off the school bus. No-mercy style. Pow, one to the head," he threatened, using his fingers to imitate that of a gun.

"Noooo! Not my baby. I'll do anything for my baby!" she whimpered, her big swollen lips drooling as if she had gotten shot up with Novocain.

"Aiight then." He took the bullets out of one of the guns and handed it to her. "I want you to beat this nigga in his head until he dies. I wanna see you bash his shit in, and then that will determine if I'mma kill you and yo kid or not. Right now, all you muthafuckas dead in my mind." He smacked her on the back of the head.

She damn near fell forward on top of Red. "Why I gotta do this shit, J.T.? I ain't have nothing to do with what y'all had going on. Now you wanna make me kill my baby daddy. That ain't right," she cried with her eyes closed.

Red looked up at her with the hole on his forehead pooling blood. "This shit ain't cool, man. I'm tellin' you, I ain't rip you off. That nigga lyin'." He sounded like he was losing his strength.

"Where you get that money in the freezer from then, huh? I buss every move wit you. I know how much every one of them mafuckas s'pose to be holdin'. So, explain to me why you got all this cake in there?"

He groaned, "I been savin' for a minute now. Tryna get my peoples outta this hood, man. This ain't no place to raise a family."

He broke into a fit of coughs, and then up came a huge glob of blood, reddish-yellow. I had to turn my head to get rid of the nausea that threatened to overtake me. Everything within eyesight was starting to smell horrible, like sweat and shit. I think his baby mother had shit on herself or something, because the room smelled like somebody was holding a shitty pamper up to a fan that was on high.

"Red, just tell him the truth, that way we ain't gotta worry about him killing us. Tell him we didn't know it was gon' be that much money and he was gon' get his cut later. We wasn't gone cut him all the way out," she cried, with snot running from her nose.

"Shut up, bitch! Shut up right now and quit all that mafuckin' lyin'! That money in there ain't got shit to do with J.T.!"

J.T.'s eyes got so big that the skin on his head moved backwards. "Bitch nigga, you just gon' keep on lyin' right in front of my face, huh?"

"I ain't lyin'. This bitch don't know what she talkin' about. She just…"

Crackk!

Molly swung the gun and bashed him upside the head with it. She swung it again and the handle landed in his eye. "You gone get me killed! I'm tired of yo shit!" she screamed, with tears flowing down her cheeks.

I took two steps back as his blood began flying into the air like a sprinkler. Every time she brought the gun down against his skull, it sounded like metal hitting bone. His face looked like somebody had thrown a red snow cone on it, the ice being his brain matter, and the juice being his blood. I stared, mesmerized and scared at the same time.

"That's what I'm talkin' about. Kill that nigga! Kill 'em!" J.T. hollered, looking more excited than I had ever seen him before in my life. He was hunched over, cheering her on. His top lip curled up. "Beat that nigga shit in!"

Red laid in a pool of his own blood, looking helpless. I almost wanted to tell her to stop, but I knew J.T. would lose his mind.

While she continued to beat him in the head, J.T. held up his phone recording her. "I'm gon' get high as a muthafucka and watch this back," he said, licking his thick lips.

After Molly saw Red was no longer moving, she looked down on him with her whole face covered in his blood. She looked like Carrie did in that Stephen King movie. She straddled him and ran her hand across her face to wipe some of the blood away.

J.T. pulled her up by her hair. "Aiight, bitch! That nigga is dead." He leaned down and put his fingers to his neck. Stood up and put the pistol to her head. "Now you finna be."

Her eyes got bucked and she fell to her knees. "Please don't do this, J.T. Please don't kill me. I done everything you said do. I swear, I won't say nothing," she begged, looking up at him.

He took a step back and pressed the gun harder to her forehead. "Bitch, that ain't how we get down in Compton. It's blood in, blood out."

She shook her head. "My son, J.T. Please save me for my son. He needs me." She crawled to him and wrapped her arm around his leg like a little kid.

I got to feeling some type of way. I didn't like how the whole scene looked. I mean, she did everything he had asked of her. I didn't feel like there was any reason for him to kill her. She had a son to live for.

J.T. looked over to me. "Lil' Momma, go start the car in the alley. I'mma finish this bitch, and I'll be out there in a minute," he said, staring at her like he hated her guts.

She looked up at him with the fear of death in her eyes. "J.T., I swear I won't say nothing. My son is my everything. He's the only one that means anything to me. You let me live and I will dedicate my life to you. I will never forget how you spared me," she offered. "All I have is my little boy."

J.T. bit into his bottom lip, looking like he was ready to buss his gat. "Nawl, fuck that, shorty. I gotta body you. That's how the game go." He closed his eyes a little bit, ready to shoot.

I prepared for the loud noise and at the same time, pulled his arm back. "Nawl, baby, don't do it! Please!" I hollered, standing in front of her. The truth was, I didn't know her from Adam, but I kept imagining her kid getting off the school bus and J.T. killing him, too. I didn't want that on my conscience, especially since I knew I could prevent it. He would probably whoop my ass later, but I had to save this chick. I just had to.

"Baby, get the fuck out the way before I whoop yo ass, I'm not playin'. I told you how the game go. You just s'pose to be a spectator, not in the middle of the field wit me right now." He grabbed me by the shirt and threw me on the couch.

He aimed the gun back at Molly. "This bitch know who you is. She know who I am. Why should I risk this bitch talkin' to somebody?"

"She can't say shit, J.T. You recorded her killing him. What can she possibly say?"

"I wouldn't have said nothing if he didn't do that. I ain't no snitch, and I don't play about my son. That nigga, Red, ain't honor my baby, so I enjoyed killing his ass. I took way too many beatings from him anyway." She wiped more blood from her forehead. "J.T., you spare my life, I'll put you on a lick so cold, you'll never have to worry about no money for a long time. I'll do that, and I'll be in debt to you. I know I'm supposed to be dead right now." She blinked back tears. "All I'm asking for is a chance."

He looked over at me and shook his head. "Lil' Momma, if this shit come back to bite me in the ass, I'll never forgive you." He lowered the gun. "Y'all help me get his ass taken care of before yo son get home. We got a lot of burnin' to do."

Ghost

Chapter 2
Jennifer

I felt him grab me by the hair, snapping my neck backward so hard, it felt like he was trying to pull my head off.

"You stupid bitch. I'm tired of you actin' like you sick all the time. Every time I wanna fuck, alla sudden you sick! Fuck this!" He flung me to the floor and ripped my nightgown down the middle, exposing my Victoria's Secret purple bra and panty set.

"Get off me, Bobby! I'm really sick. I been throwing up all day long. I think I got the flu!"

Whap! He open-handedly smacked me across the face and ripped my bra off me. It wasn't easy for him to do, but he kept at it. Yanking so hard, causing my body to jerk up and down off the ground, until the material ripped, exposing my titties.

As soon as they were out, his mouth was all over them, sucking on my nipples so hard and rough, it felt like he was trying to rip them off of my breasts. He trailed his hand down into my panties, trying to force my sex lips apart with his fingers.

"Open these mafuckas up!" he moaned into my ear loudly. "I gotta get me some of this half-breed pussy. You got the best Indian pussy I ever had, and I'm 'bout to enjoy me some of it right now."

He ripped my panties down my legs and off my feet. Once off, he hopped between my legs, pulled his dick through his boxer hole and rubbed the head up against my sex lips.

I pushed at his chest, but to no avail. It seemed like the more I tried to pry him off me, the more excited he got. "Please get off me, Bobby. I'm tired and I don't want to do this right now."

I felt him find my opening and my reluctant gates opened to welcome his uninvited ten inches deep within me. I closed my eyes, trying my best to ignore the pain of his assault.

He pounded into me at full speed. "Oh, shit yeah. Man, this pussy good! Damn, Jennifer, you got the best pussy in the world, baby!"

It never took him long to come. As if on cue, I felt his body tense up. All at once, he started to shake, releasing his unwanted seed inside me, while tears rolled down my eyes.

I laid there on the floor with my legs wide open. Once again, he had taken advantage of me, and I had allowed him to do so. I was so tired of being on the receiving end of his assaults.

Slowly, I closed my legs and started to get up. I could smell the sex in the air and it was making me sick on the stomach. Before he'd had his way with me, I was already feeling flu-like symptoms. I mean, while it was true that I often made up excuses to avoid us sleeping together, this time I was actually telling the truth. I crawled to my feet, bending to pick my panties up off the floor. I felt his semen oozing down my leg and it sickened me even more.

Bobby readjusted his boxers with a big smile on his face. "Ooo-whee! That was just what I needed right there, baby. You got me feelin' like a boss for real. You see, now was that so bad?" he asked, smacking me on the ass, startling me.

When I felt the slap, I felt the tears escape me. He just didn't get it. I had been with him ever since I was sixteen years old and he'd taken my virginity. He'd promised me that once I gave it to him, he would make me feel like a princess for the rest of my life, but every word of it was a lie. Ever since I had allowed him to put his dick inside of me, he'd treated as nothing more than a tool to get him off. That, and a punching bag. It didn't take long before I hated his guts with all of my might.

"Get yo ass in there and make me somethin' to eat. That good pussy got me all kinds of hungry. So, I want you to throw down as only you can." He grabbed me and wrapped me into his arms. I tried to fight him off of me. "Come on now, Bobby, I don't feel like it. Get off of me." I pushed him, and he flew into the wall. I figured he had to be drunk, because I didn't push him that hard.

His back hit the wall and then he fell to his ass, before bouncing up like a basketball. "Bitch, I know you ain't just do what I think you did." Before I could answer him, he was flying at me full speed, until he closed the gap and slapped the taste out of my mouth. I tasted blood right away as I flew into the wall and bit my tongue.

He grabbed me by the hair and slapped me again, this time a lot harder than before. *Whisp!* I tried to cover my face, but it didn't do any good because he was slapping me again. "Bobby, please stop!" I yelled, before he pulled me to the floor and got on top of me.

"You half-breed bitch, you just don't get it, do you? You belong to me. If I wanna whoop yo ass every muthafucking day until you know shit ain't a game, then that's what I'mma do. I'm tired of you taking me through all of this bullshit, so I'm about to kick all of the fight out of yo Indian ass!" He slurred, and for the first time, I could smell the alcohol on his breath, along with the shitty stench that was always there. I tried to hump my hips upward to buck him off of me, but it didn't help my cause one bit, because he stayed put and slapped me again, this time knocking my head into the floor. I felt dizzy. I could also feel the blood running down my neck.

"Please! You don't have to beat me no more," I whimpered, praying that he would get off of me. I felt dizzy.

I could also feel the blood running down my neck. "Please! You don't have to beat me no more," I whimpered, praying that he would get off of me.

He grabbed me by the neck and squeezed. "Bitch, I'll kill you if you ever play wit me again. You are my slave. You have no say-so on your life anymore. You remember, yo dope-fiend-ass momma sold you to me for an ounce of meth? That means you my property, and I'm the only one that love yo stankin' ass!" He squeezed my neck even harder. I couldn't breathe and in that moment, I wanted for him to kill me because everything he was saying was true.

My mother had sold me to him when I was only sixteen years old for an ounce of meth. He was already thirty. Before that time, me and my mother had been very close.

I never understood what made her just up and give me away to him the way she did, and I never asked her. I think it was because I was too afraid of what her answer might have been. But then again, my mother was all screwed up after she'd developed a habit to meth when I was just twelve years old and my father left home. My mother was Native American, and my father was black. Her dating my father was already extremely taboo in the eyes of her family.

As soon as they found out whom she was spending time with on or off the reservation, they kicked her out and she landed right in his lap. She was only fifteen herself and he was all she knew. When he left our family for another, even younger female, my mother turned to drugs, and things had gone downhill ever since.

"Bobby, okay, baby. Just let me go and cook. I won't give you any more problems, I promise." He stood up and took a few steps back. "Aiight then, get yo ass up and get in that kitchen. This shit ain't a game, and you betta stop playing wit me like it is one. I'll kill you in this mafucka! You understand me?" he asked, grabbing my long hair and yanking my head backward. I hated when he did this. It made me feel less than human, plus, it hurt like a bitch.

"Yes, I understand."

He kicked me in the ass, and I walked into the kitchen with tears rolling down my face. "What do you wanna eat?" I whimpered, sniffing the snot back up into my nose.

"I got a taste for some fried chicken and white rice. Make it happen." He stretched his arms over his head and yawned. "I'm so tired of kickin' yo monkey ass. Damn, you too fine for me to be fuckin' yo face up like that. Don't you get tired of me beatin' yo ass? I mean, damn, it seems like every single day I'm whoopin' yo ass for something new when all you gotta do is fall in line and stop making shit so hard. The sooner you understand that you belong to me, the sooner I can put these hands up" He shook his head. "Stupid yellow bitch."

I could feel my scalp throbbing where he'd damn near pulled my hair from my scalp. My neck hurt, and most of all, my pride and feelings were hurt. I felt like less than a woman. I didn't feel like a human being, and that is how I felt every single time he took advantage of me.

I opened the refrigerator and looked inside. There was no chicken. I opened the freezer and went over the meats we had and once again, I could not locate any chicken. I was starting to panic. I swallowed and took a deep breath. "Bobby, it ain't no chicken in here. Do you want me to make you something else?" I asked in the most submissive voice I could master.

He stormed into the kitchen, bumping me out of the way. "I know you done lost yo muthafuckin' mind. It better be some chicken in here, because that's what I got a taste for." He opened the refrigerator door wide and looked inside of it for a long time, before slamming it so hard that it twisted to the side a little bit. *Whoom!* "Bitch, you betta tell me why it ain't no chicken in this house, when I specifically told you I wanted me some chicken yesterday." I backed away from him as he made his way toward me.

I was scared and worried about what he was going to do to me. "Bobby, I'm sorry. I'll go out right now and get some for you, baby. I just thought we had some here, that's all," I said, bumping my back into the wall.

He walked right into my face and curled his upper lip. "When was the last time you went shopping?" he asked, with both of his arms outstretched on each side of my head, while he breathed in my face.

His breath smelled horrible. It smelled like a bunch of people with stinky feet had their shoes off in his mouth, wiggling their toes. "Baby, I had plans on going this weekend when I get more money on my Food Share card."

"Okay, but when did I tell you to go grocery shopping?" He frowned up his face and looked at the ceiling as if he was growing impatient.

"You told me to go yesterday, but how could I when I don't have any money?" He grabbed me by the throat. "Oh, now you trying to say I don't know how to take care of my woman? You callin' me a dead beat?" He flung me to the floor so hard, the side of my face bounced off of it. I felt him grabbing me by the hair, and something told me to elbow him, so I did. Then I jumped up and started to run for dear life, with my heart beating so fast it hurt.

"You yellow bitch, get yo ass back here!" he screamed, holding his face. I struggled with the lock on the front door. I had unlocked the door a million times, but now all of a sudden, I was forgetting exactly how to do it.

By the time I figured it out, I was being thrown to the floor and he was on top of me slapping me across the face so hard, I bit my tongue. "Bobby, no!" *Slap!*

"I done told you about that running shit, didn't I?" *Slap!* I felt the sting of his hand connecting with my skin and it hurt so bad, I wanted to die.

I knew what came next and I was not ready for it to happen. I felt him try to get my clothes off of me, and something in me made me knee him in the nuts. *Crunch!*

His face turned a shade of blue. He closed his eyes and then fell off of me. "You fuckin' bitch. I'm gon' kill you. I swear to God I am…"

I ran back into the kitchen, and pulled open the utility drawer, rifling through it until I found the hammer with the wooden handle. As soon as I found it, I ran back into the living room, where he was laid on his side with both of his hands between his legs, struggling to breathe.

I looked down on him with hatred. The more he moved around on that floor the more I hated the fact he was alive. I hated him for beating me. I hated him for raping me. I hated my mother for selling me to him. I hated myself for allowing him to take advantage of me for so long. I hated I had been so weak.

"You know what, Bobby, I hate you!" I screamed and brought the hammer down on the side of his head with all of my might. It connected with his skull and punched a hole into it. *Vomp!*

"Arrrgh, bitch! What the fuck is wrong wit you?"

I lifted the hammer over my head again and brought it back down, connecting with the side of his forehead. Once again, it put a big hole right where I'd slammed it. "I hate you, Bobby. I hate you for hurtin' me!"

"Noooo! Jennifer, please stop! I'm sorry, baby. Can't you see that I love you? Stopppp!" he hollered.

Vomp! Vomp! Vomp! I brought the hammer down again and again. Every time I did, blood sprayed across my face and some into my mouth. The thought of killing him and the feeling of finally fighting for myself, felt good. I didn't care that I was taking a life, because mine had been lost a long, long time ago. I was tired of feeling weak. I was tired of being bullied by him and everybody in my life. It was time I stood up for myself.

I grabbed the handle with two hands and brought it down into his face with all of my might. *Vomp!* A chunk of meat flew across the floor, because I had turned the hammer around and was now using the part that extracted the nails. *Vomp!* I slammed it down again and this time it got caught in his eye. I yanked, and his eye came out on the metal. I felt a sense of power.

"I hate you, Bobby! I hate you, Momma! I hate all of you for hurting me!" Before I knew it, I was down on my knees bashing his head in, when I heard a car door slam outside.

"Holy shit, that can't be nobody but Liz," I said to myself. "Fuck, what am I going to do?" I stood up and looked down on Bobby. He was a bloody mess. His face was caved in and it looked like it had been run over by a semi-truck. I could not help smiling. No more would I have to deal with his punk ass.

Thinking quickly, I grabbed him by the legs and pulled him from the living room all the way to the kitchen, then I waited on the side of the front door for Liz to step through it. I never liked her anyway. She'd stood by one too many times and watched while Bobby had beaten my head in. She was often the enabler, and I hated her nearly as much as I hated his guts.

She came through the door and for some reason, she laughed to herself. "Honey, I'm home!"

I didn't know who she was talking to, but either way it seemed odd whether it was directed at me or Bobby. I shrugged my shoulders. I waited for her to close the door before I jumped out at her. As soon as she saw me, she damn near jumped out of her skin.

"Fuck, you scared the shit out of me, bitch! Don't be doing no shit like that. I should have my brother kick yo dumb ass. Silly broad." She shook her head and proceeded to walk past me. She didn't move more than five paces when she stopped and put her hands to her mouth. "Oh my God, where is all this blood from?" She turned around to look at me.

I shook my head. "I hate you so much, Liz. You ain't been nothin' but a fuckin' bully ever since high school. I should have done this a long time ago." *Voom!* I swung the hammer and it smashed right into her left eye and got stuck. A big ass squirt of blood flew so high, it hit the ceiling.

"Aaawwww shit!" she yelled and turned around to run. I ran and tackled her simple ass to the floor, straddling her and wiggling the hammer out of her eye. "Bitch, you let him beat me every single day. You allowed him to treat me like shit. I don't know why you did the things you did to me, but now you're gonna pay. Everybody that has ever hurt me is going to pay!"

Vomp! Vomp! Vomp! I slammed the hammer into her face again and again with both hands. She was another demon that had taken ahold of me, ever since Bobby had become a part of my life. She was a pain only death could cure. I brought the hammer down again and again, until her head was mangled. It looked like a melted Halloween mask somebody had poured a bunch of ketchup on. Her body laid there. Lifeless.

I went and took a nice long shower as tears of pain coursed down my cheek. It was finally over. I had got my life back.

Ghost

Chapter 3
Lil' Momma

"Well, baby, I'll see you tomorrow. You betta be going right back home, too. Don't let me find out you're out here trying to mess with some other female, because if I do, we gon' have a problem," I said, leaning over my seat so I could kiss him on his juicy ass lips.

We were parked in front of my parents' house and I was a little afraid to go inside because I knew that it was about to be a bunch of bullshit as soon as I walked through the door.

It was three in the morning and I could see my father's plumber's truck in the driveway, which meant that he was home, and probably waiting for me to get there. I took a deep breath as I stared out the window at the house.

J.T. mugged the house. "You know you ain't gotta go in there, right? I mean, you could stroll back to the crib wit me and not have to worry about them today."

I shook my head and let out another sigh. "Yeah, I wish it was that easy, but my people crazy. If I don't go in there right now, it's gonna be all kinds of drama when I finally do get there. I might as well go in here and get this over with. I can't run forever." J.T. curled his upper lip as if he were getting angry.

"Baby, it ain't like you a kid no more. You're in yo twenties now. They still treating you like you still in high school or something. It's time you break away from the nest and get on some grown people shit. That's the only way they gon' respect you." He sat back in his seat and squeezed my thigh. "Here come yo punk-ass father right now too."

I turned my head so fast to look out the window, I heard it pop. Sure enough, there was my father coming down the stairs off of our porch with his robe wrapped around him. He had a menacing look on his face. I knew there was about to be trouble. He walked up to the car and pulled the passenger's door open, nearly making me fall out of it. I found myself halfway in the car and halfway out of it.

J.T. jumped out of the car immediately and ran around to the side I was sitting on. I watched him push my father away from my door, then he leaned down and picked me up. "You okay, Lil' Momma?" As he asked this question, he was looking at my father with anger in his eyes.

My father, a heavyset short man, with an afro that was all bald in the middle, walked up on J.T. and bumped his chest against his. "Muthafucka, that's my daughter right there. Now, you let her go or it's about to be some trouble out here tonight."

J.T. pulled me behind him and pushed my father so hard, he flew backward, tripping over his own feet. "Yo, I ain't yo kid, old man. You betta respect my gangsta, or else I'mma beat the shit out of you, Blood. And you ain't about to be putting yo hands on her in front of me neither. Yo wife in the house and not out here. This my woman!"

I watched my father start to make his way to his feet. J.T. went under his shirt, and I knew he was going to grab a gun, so I stepped in front of him and wrapped my arms around his neck. "Baby, please don't shoot him. Just let me go into the house and I'll make this all better. Please, we don't need no more trouble for one day," I begged, with my voice sounding whiny.

My father held up his guards like he really wanted to fight. "Come on, you son of a bitch. You wanna fuck wit me and stand in the way of how I discipline my daughter? Come on!" He bounced on his toes like he was ready to go to war with J.T.

J.T. frowned and then smiled. "Ah yeah, that's what you wanna do?" He took the pistol off of his waist and threw it on the driver's seat of his car. "Yo, I'm about to whoop you, old dude, just to show you that this ain't that. You think just 'cuz you can beat a woman, you can fuck in my business? Alright, well let me put this Crenshaw ass whoopin' on that ass one time, for the one time."

I tried to wrap him in my arms, but he pushed me off of him, and I leaned against the car. I watched him jog up to my father with his guards up. My father swung a haymaker. J.T. ducked and came back up with a hook that crashed against my father's cheek and knocked him to the ground.

"Yeah, let's go, old man. I aint no woman, it's gon' take a whole lot to whoop my ass." He took three steps back and bounced on his toes, waiting on my father to get up. "Come on and get yo ass up and take this ass whoopin' like a man!"

My mother came out of the house with her nightgown on, and a robe wrapped mostly around her. As soon as she saw what was going on, she ran off the porch, right in front of my father. "Marvin, get in the house! You ain't got nothin' to prove to this street punk! Lil' Momma, get yo ass in the house too, before somebody call the police and yo father be back in jail. Is that what you want?" she asked, with tears coming down her cheeks.

I shook my head as I walked over to J.T. and grabbed his arm. "Baby, please give him a G-pass. Let him go on this one. You already know he can't fuck in yo business. I know you was just protecting me, but I'll be alright." I stepped on my tippy toes and kissed him on the cheek.

He wrapped his arms around me the whole time, mugging my father. He kissed my lips, and slid his tongue into my mouth, both of us putting on a scene in front of them. I knew it was going to get me in serious trouble as soon as I went into

33

the house, but in that moment, I really didn't care. I just wanted to make sure my man was happy, and he would leave before he killed my father.

"I'll see you in the morning, baby, I promise." I hugged him one more time, and then reluctantly let him go.

He was about to get into the car when he paused. "If I find out he put his hands on you tonight, on everything I love, on my blood, I'mma kill that nigga." After saying that, he got into his cherry-red Lexus, and stormed away from the curb.

As soon as I got into the house, my father snatched me up and pinned me against the wall. "Bitch, you had the audacity to let yo nigga put his hands on me in front of your mother, like I'm some bitch or something? Who the fuck do you think you are? You stay in my muthafucking house. You're under my roof, which means that I own yo ass in every way, shape, form and fashion."

I tried to push him out of my face. "Daddy, let me go. I didn't know that you and he was about to get into it. You can't always run up on him, if you don't want him standing up for himself. He thought you was about to beat me outside, that's the only reason that he stepped in," I said as he pushed me against the wall even more.

He put his forehead against mine. "Bitch, don't you know that you are my daughter? I can do anything to you I want to, because I rule yo muthafucking ass." He kissed me on the lips and I tried to turn my head, but he grabbed my chin into his fingers and held my face in place, kissing my lips again, sucking on them loudly.

I started to shake, and I said a silent prayer in my head hoping it would stop what I knew what was about to take place.

"Daddy, please let me go to bed. I'm tired and I really need to get some sleep," I whimpered.

He licked my lips and railed his hands around until he was cupping my booty.

"Now all of a sudden, you're sleepy. You wasn't sleepy when you were kissing all over him, now was you? Was you sleepy when you were bringing yo ass in this house at damn near three in the morning?"

I felt him trail his hand all the way under my butt, until they were in my crease rubbing my mound. Once again, I tried to push him away. "I'm tired, Daddy, please just let me go to sleep," I begged.

He bit into my neck and then sucked loudly. "You already know that the more you fight me, the better this pussy is for me. It makes it that much more taboo, and it turns me on all the more."

"But, Daddy, I'm sorry. I promise I'll listen to you from now on. You don't have to do this. Please."

He flipped me around and pushed my face against the wall. I felt him reach around me and unzip my pants before yanking them down my legs. As soon as they were down, he yanked my thong panties down next, and stuck his face between my ass cheeks, taking his tongue and licking in between them loudly.

"Umm, this is what it's all about right here. This the only reason that boy is protecting you like he is. It's because you got this fat ass booty back here. You too damn slim to have an ass this fat. That's why I gotta suck all over it too." He took my ass cheeks and spread them, holding me open for himself. I felt his tongue go deep in me, and then he was sucking on my sex lips, rolling my clitoris with his thumb, trying to turn me on.

"Momma, can you please come and get your husband! Please, Momma!" I yelled and waited to see if I would hear her footsteps coming to save me, but she never came.

In my whole life, she had never saved me from him. My biological father had passed away when I was only seven years old, after battling colon cancer for three years. Ever since then, her new husband had been going in on me, and she had never done anything about it.

He picked me up and threw me across the bed, before straddling me. He pulled my shirt up, and unlatched my bra from the front.

My breasts spilled out into his hands. "Look at these pretty titties. Why would anybody need more than an A-cup? Looks like you gon' stay young forever, baby, and I'm gon' enjoy you every single day for as long as I can." He leaned down and sucked my whole right breast into his mouth, and pulled on my left nipple so hard, I winced in pain.

"Stopppp! Get off me! Momma, come get your husband. He's raping me!" I screamed.

He sat up and slapped me across the face. "Shut up, bitch! Yo momma don't give a fuck what goes on between me and you, just as long as I stay with her. You the only reason we been together this long. It's because of what you got between these lil' thighs right here."

I felt his fingers slide over my naked sex lips, before parting them. He threw my thighs apart and got between them, put my left leg on his shoulder, and then I felt him enter me violently. Slamming himself home, pulling all the way out and implanting his manhood in me all over again. I could feel the tears flowing down my cheeks. I wanted to die. I felt so low, and so alone.

The bed started to go haywire with the springs screeching and squeaking loudly. I knew my mother had to hear them, because her bedroom was right next to my own. I wondered how a mother could sit back and allow for her child to be violated.

I also wondered how I had stayed so long. Even though my mother hurt me by never protecting me, I felt that if I left that house, he would surely kill her. So, there I was, the sacrifice for their relationship, and most times I wondered if she even cared.

He threw my other leg on his shoulder and now he was really going at me. I felt him beating down my walls. The headboard was slamming into the wall like crazy. He was breathing hard in my face, and licking my tears away. "I love this pussy right here. You're my daughter, and my baby got the best pussy in the world. This shit still tight. After all these years, you still got that snapper!" he growled, speeding up the pace.

I felt him start to tense up and that let me know he was seconds away from coming. I did not want his seed in my body again. I hated this man for what he was doing to me, and what he had been doing to me ever since I was twelve years old. "Get off of me!" I screamed, sat up and started punching him in the face, neck, and everywhere I could reach from that position. I took my nails and scratched him across the face and finally, he let me go.

"Arrrrggh, you bitch!" he hollered, and fell off of me with his hard dick sticking up in the air. I pushed him with all of my might and he flew off of the bed onto his side, with his hands over his face.

"I'm tired of you raping me every day, Daddy. You're not supposed to do me like that. I'm your fucking kid!" I screamed. I searched on the floor until I found my panties. As soon as I did, I slowly slid them up my legs, and made a run for the door. As soon as I got it open, I saw he was getting to his feet.

Ghost

"Get your ass back here, Lil' Momma. This shit ain't over. I ain't came yet and until I do, you gon' have a fucked-up morning. You can bet yo bottom dollar on that!" he hollered.

"Momma! Momma! Momma, where you at? I need you, he's trying to rape me again!" I said, jiggling the knob on her bedroom door. I could not believe it was locked. Didn't she hear me screaming for her?

I felt my father behind me, and then he slung me to the floor. "Anne, get out here and help me hold her down until I come! Get yo ass out here right now, before I snap the fuck out!" he yelled.

My mother's door flew open so fast, the knob on the door slammed into the wall and left a big hole in it. I couldn't believe she would jump through a hoop, just because he had said so.

She came out of the room and dropped to her knees. "What do you want me to do, baby, just tell me?"

"Hold the bitch arms, dat way she can't scratch me up no more," he said, getting between my legs, after ripping my thong away violently. "Hurry up, too."

I closed my eyes as I felt my mother grab ahold of my wrists and squeeze them so tight that after a while, I started to lose feeling in my hands.

Tears sailed down my cheeks as he went in and out of my body. I felt so sick and so vulnerable. I felt like the world hated me and I had been put there to suffer nothing but pain. The more he grunted into my face, and every ounce of pain he caused between my legs, made me no longer care about my mother's well-being.

I hated her in that moment. I hated her because she had allowed for him to abuse me for as long I could remember. I hated her for being such a coward. I hated him for taking advantage of a defenseless child, and a weak woman. He was

38

a rapist, lower than scum in my book, and I knew that as soon as he got done doing his business, I was going to find a way to make him pay, because I was tired of the abuse. I was tired of the assaults and having a mother that really wasn't a mother. She no longer meant anything to me.

"I'm coming, Anne. Awwww shit, I'm coming in this hot ass pussy. I love you so much, baby. Come here." He grabbed her by the head and they began to make out, while I cried beneath them.

Afterwards, he grabbed me by the hair and stuck his fat face into my slender one. "Don't you ever deny me this body. You belong to me and I ain't gon' keep on telling you that. Whenever I want some of this shit, I'm gone get it, because that's what a father supposed to do with his baby girl. It's been like that since the beginning of time. If you ever deny me again, I'm gon' kill you. I'm gon' kill you in cold blood right after I fuck yo brains out because this shit ain't a game. You understand that?"

I blinked tears. "Yes, Daddy, I do."

Ghost

Chapter 4
Jennifer

I stood there in the shower, allowing the warm water to beat against my face. It felt good and I was trying my best to focus on how good it actually felt, and not the fact that I had two dead bodies in the living room. A part of me wanted to freak out so bad, but for some reason, I just couldn't. I mean, I was absolutely terrified about what was going to take place, because I didn't really have a clue. The unknown always spooked me, but the fact that Bobby was no longer alive was doing something to my brain and had me in a state of euphoria.

I finished shampooing the blood out of my hair, and watched it pool down the drain by my foot. I would no longer have to deal with them. I would no longer have to worry about how Bobby was going to hurt me. That was all that mattered. And his sister, well, I felt she got what she deserved just as well.

After cleaning up the bathroom, and getting myself together as best I could, I stepped out into the living room to assess the situation. I shook my head after looking over the bloody mess. I mean, there was blood and brain matter everywhere. It looked like a horror movie or something, and the smell was putrid.

Bobby's head was smashed all the way in, flattened. He was missing an eye, and a thick river of blood slowly oozed from the socket. His mouth was wide open, and I knew that if he still had life inside of him, he would have been running it a mile a minute.

His sister's head looked identical to his, yet her body was twisted slightly different. Where Bobby was laid on his back, his sister was laid on her side, with her head smashed into the floor. It looked like it had been melted into it.

I tried to think of the first things to do to get everything in order and I couldn't come up with anything. I thought about burning the house down. Maybe I would get away with everything then. I didn't know when we were set to have any visitors, but Bobby's sister did have a coworker that came over every morning to pick her up, and she was a very nosey woman. I figured if she didn't hear from Liz in a couple of days, she would have somebody knock on the door, because that's just how she was.

So, as I knelt down looking over the bodies, I started to panic because I didn't want to go to prison. I called my cousin, Lil' Momma, and she picked up her phone on the third ring.

"Hey Jen, what you doin' calling me so late?" I asked, whispering into the phone.

"I know, I know. I should have texted you first, but I needed to hear your voice. I got a crazy dilemma on my hands, and I need some help." I looked over the scene again and now I really started to panic, because it was like my reality was starting to slap me in the face. Holy fuck, this was two dead bodies. Bodies of people I had killed in cold blood. My life was over.

"Nawl, you good. Tell me what's the matter?" Once again, she was whispering. It sounded like her voice was breaking up some, like she'd been crying.

"Okay, before I do that, what's the matter with you?" I asked, standing up. A roach crawled across the wall with a big egg hanging out of its ass. It looked like it was close to falling off of the wall. I took my house shoe off of my foot and smashed it. *Damn, now I done killed three things in one day,* I thought.

"I'm okay, but Marvin did do it to me again. This time, he hurt me real bad down there, and my mother helped him." She began sniveling on the other end of the phone.

"What!" I slid my house shoe back onto my foot, and gripped my phone so hard, it hurt my hand. I had to loosen my grip a little bit. "What do you mean she helped him, Lil' Momma?"

Now, she was sobbing loudly. I could hear her trying to catch her breath. "She, she held me down while he did his thing. I had gotten away from him and tried to get into her room to safety, but she locked the door. Then, when he told her to come out and hold me down, she did it, and didn't let me go until he was finished. I hate both of them so much, Cousin," she cried loudly. "I don't understand why they would do that to me."

I plopped down on the floor, sitting Indian-style. Damn, how could a girl's mother hold her down, while her husband raped her daughter? I could not even fathom what she was going through mentally right now.

Lil' Momma was my favorite cousin. I loved her with all of me, and I would die for her in a heartbeat. Growing up, we were more like sisters than cousins. Her father and my father were brothers, so we were pretty much raised together. The girls used to pick on me in school because they said I thought I was better than them because of how pretty I was. And Lil' Momma was just as fine, but they picked on her because when we were younger, she was very slim. So, they called her all kinds of nasty names relating to anorexia. One thing about her being small, it never stopped her from kicking their ass. I had seen her whoop two girls at one time before. Once she started crying and closed her eyes, all bets were off.

She would get knee-deep into some ass. Most times when a female jumped into her fights, I never had to help. I usually had to help them by pulling her off of them.

"Baby, where are they now?" I asked, trying to sound as consoling as possible.

She sniffed the air loudly, I imagined to pull her snot back into her nostrils. "They're in their bedroom making love. I can hear them clear as day. I hate their guts, Cousin. I wish I was dead right now, so I wouldn't have to go through all of this pain." She cried for a little while, and then stopped.

"I feel exactly how you feel when Bobby does his thing to you. I feel violated, and sick. And now they're in there celebrating because of what he did."

That blew my mind. I hoped that she was exaggerating. I couldn't imagine Anne doing something like that with her husband, but then again, I was not in the house with them.

I figured Lil' Momma would know the things they did on a regular basis more than me. "Lil' Momma, I got rid of Bobby." The words left my mouth so fast, I didn't realize what I had said until it was too late to take them back.

I could hear her inhale sharply. "What you mean, you got rid of him?"

"I was so tired of him puttin' his fuckin' hands on me, I got rid of him just like J.T. gets rid of people when he's over them." I paced back and forth with the phone to my ear. I could feel the wet liquid under my house shoes as I stepped into one blood puddle after the next, in the carpet.

Lil' Momma was silent. "If you're sayin' what I think you're sayin', then I'm scared shitless right now. I'm tryin' my best to give you the benefit of the doubt, 'cuz I just know you're not sayin' what I think you are."

"Listen! Everything you're thinkin' is absolutely right! I got rid of that asshole, and I don't feel no type of way about it. I'm happy he's gone, and Liz went with him." At saying this last part, I lowered my voice.

"Holy shit! Where are you?" she asked, sounding concerned.

"I'm at home with them, and I'm freakin' out 'cuz I don't know what to do. I don't want to go to jail. I won't be able to make it in there by myself. It'd be a different thing if you were right beside me."

"Jennifer, look, calm down. I'm going to call J.T. and have him come over there to get you. If there is anybody that knows what to do in these situations, it's him. So, let me give him a jingle, and I'll make sure he's at your house in no time. I promise."

No more than thirty minutes later, there was a knock on my door. I answered it and as soon as I saw J.T., I crashed into him, wrapping my arms around his neck. "J.T., I fucked up big time. I killed them. I killed both of them, just look." I lead him into the door.

Stepping into the front room, you could smell their blood in the air. It smelled like burnt metal, with a hint of feces. He walked into the living room, and upon seeing Bobby, a big smile crept across his face.

"You finally executed that bitch ass nigga. Good for you. Who is that bitch over there though?" he asked, pointing at Liz's mangled body.

"That was Liz. I hated her because she always allowed him to jump on me. Sometimes, she even added fuel to the fire, just so he could really fuck me up. I was tired of both of them, so I snapped, and that's what happened." I lowered my head, praying he wouldn't hate me for what I had did to them.

He walked up to me and pulled me into his arms, kissing me on the forehead. He held me so tight, I felt safe and secure in his arms. "Yo, you good from now on, Ma. I got you. Fuck both of them. Ain't nobody gon' find out about this shit, because I'm finna show you how to get rid of the bodies. I love that you got this killer shit in you too. That makes me feel some type of way about yo ass." He kissed me again on the forehead and held me tighter, before letting me go.

"Okay, so what am I going to do?" I looked down at their bodies and saw that Liz's was already starting to swell up. It looked like she was about to pop.

"Don't even trip, I'll be right back," he said, jogging out of the house. Two minutes later, he came back inside with a duffel bag. He sat it on the floor, and unzipped it. "First thing we gon' do is cut they arms and legs off. Then once we do that, we gon' put them in the bathtub, while I pour this blue acid on them with this ammonia. The ammonia gon' help the acid to not eat away at the porcelain of your tub. We gotta rub the ammonia all around the basin in the inside, before we pour this blue acid in there. Once our liquid's ready, then we gon' put they limbs in there one at a time, and that shit gon' eat 'em up. All that flesh gon' leave the bone and deteriorate. All we'll be left with is fragile bone, and we gon' smash that shit to dust, and pour it out in the river."

I was looking at him with my eyes as big as paper plates.

He was talking about everything like it wasn't a big deal and that was blowing my mind, and having me intrigued at the same time. "Okay, so just tell me what to do."

I held down Bobby's leg, while J.T. put the big ax over his head and brought it down with so much velocity, it chopped his leg right away from the bone. It separated, and I damn near jumped up and ran away. Blood splattered onto my face.

"Alright, push that mafucka to the side over there and grab his other one," he said, breathing hard with a slight smile on his face. I did just what he asked me to do, order for order, and before it was too long, we had a pile of limbs and body parts in one pile of the floor in my basement. J.T. and I carried them one at a time, up the stairs and into the bathroom, where he lowered them into the tub, and the acid ate away the flesh almost immediately. It bubbled up and sounded like a soda pop after you'd shaken it up and twisted the top off.

After we soaked all of their limbs in the acid, J.T. took this metal rod and let the tub out. As soon as the acid drained out, their bones came into view. He had three heavy-duty, big black garbage bags that we loaded with their remains. We took all of them into the basement, and he smashed them into dust with a big sledgehammer. After that, we tied the bags into a knot and threw them in the trunk of his cherry-red Lexus.

We didn't finish cleaning the whole house until three hours later. "Yo, this that shit them crime scene clean-up men use to get rid of blood, and traces of bodily fluids. I gotta keep on spraying this shit while you scrub, until it stops turning pink, which is a bodily fluid detector. You understand?" he said, holding up two different spray bottles.

I nodded my head and continued to pay close attention.

"Aiight, now you gon' stay here with me for a little while. I can't have you over there in that house all by yourself, because trust me, you about to start having crazy ass nightmares where you see them in your dreams. That's called remorse, and all killers have it at first. Once that remorse shit get out of yo system, you gon' be able to keep it moving. Killing ain't shit. It's a part of life. Everybody gotta die, it's just a matter of when," he said, rubbing my chin with his thumb. "You okay?"

I sat there on the couch, looking up at him, trying to take in everything that he was saying. I was mesmerized by my cousin's man, because he had a certain type of swagger that was alluring to me. He carried himself like he had it all together, and the way he treated my cousin whenever I saw them together, always made me feel some type of way. I mean, I knew they had never made it a point to say they were

Ghost

exclusive, but them having feelings for each other was evident.

"I'm good, J.T. It's just been a lot that has taken place in such a short amount of time. I feel drained and a little I scared."

He sat down beside me on the couch and slid his arm around my shoulder, then he made me lay my head on his chest, pressing my head to it with his hand. "Well, if you tired then you can fall out right here, where you can hear my heartbeat. That beat is there to let you know that you got a real nigga riding for you from here on out. Ain't no bitch nigga gon' ever put his hands on you again. I got you! I wanted to body that fool Bobby a long time ago, but Lil' Momma told me to stay out of it. She told me she had hollered at you, and you told her you didn't want me getting involved, because you know how I get down. So, I had to respect that. But, I never respected that fuck nigga. Any nigga pushing forty that goes out and buys a child is a mafucka I'd like to torture." He started laughing. "But, it seemed like you got to him before I could and I gotta give you yo props on that." He kissed me on the forehead again. "Yo, we poured that nigga out in the river. He long gone, Jennifer, it's about time we move on and focus on bigger and better things, because you deserve better than what that fuck nigga was giving you."

I snuggled further into him. "Thank you for saying that, J.T. You have no idea how much I needed to hear those words. That's why Lil' Momma loves you so much."

He laid his cheek against mine. "Yeah, that's my baby right there. She loves you way more than me, and because of how much she loves you, she's willing to do anything for you, and I am too. You're a part of this family. And the love we gon' establish for each other gon' be second to none." He yawned, and laid his cheek back against mine.

48

I smiled and felt warmer than I probably should have. He had me feeling secure and protected. I felt loved, and special. I felt like he genuinely gave a fuck about me, and that had me feeling emotional because I had never experienced that from a man before.

We passed out at the same time, I guessed. A few hours later, we were awakened by the beating on his front door. I shot up, just knowing that it was the police. I imagined them throwing me in handcuffs and leading me off to prison, where some big broad weighing four hundred pounds, would sit on me and make me her bitch for the rest of my life. I felt the tears running down my cheeks, and my knees got weak.

J.T. jumped up, leaned down and slid his hand under the couch we had fallen asleep on. He came back up with a chrome pistol that had a long clip hanging out of it. He walked to the door and eyed me closely. "Get back, just in case."

I nodded and stepped out of the room, but kept him in my view. My knees were shaking so bad, I thought I would fall down. I was scared and trying to figure out how we would get out of this one. I was even passing gas on the low.

"Who is it?" he asked, with his ear to the door.

I couldn't hear what the response on the other side of the door was, but the next thing I knew, he was opening it and standing to the side.

I saw his mother pass him with her hair all over the place. She looked like she was about ready to fall over. Her lips were white and crusty, and her clothes looked so dirty, you would have sworn she had been working on cars the entire day.

"J.T., I need some money, baby, so I can pay my rent. Times is hard." She came in and sat down on the same couch we'd fallen asleep on. She didn't waste any time pulling out her pipe and sitting it on the table. Rummaging through her pockets, she came out with a plastic bag, with little rocks of crack inside of it.

J.T. stuck his head outside and looked around before closing the door. "Momma, it's too early for you to be over here begging for money. Now, you know I love you, but you gotta have a little more respect than that," he said, standing over her. He gave me a look that said he was embarrassed by what she was doing. I returned his gaze with a look of sympathy.

"Who I'm supposed to be respecting in this house? You my son, and if I wanna come over here first thing in the morning and hit you up for some money, then that's just what I'm gon' do. I had to find ways to feed you first thing in the morning when you were a kid, and I did it. Now, all of a sudden, I'm being disrespectful, because I'm catching you bright and early? Child, please." She smacked her lips, stuffed a chunk of the crack into the pipe and put fire to it, inhaling so hard that her jaws hollowed out.

She held the smoke for a few seconds and then blew it into the air. My stomach turned right away because I hated the smell of crack. That shit smelled like shitty burnt plastic.

J.T. clenched his jaw and knelt down beside her as she laid back on the couch with her eyes closed. "What I tell you about smoking this stuff, huh?"

She opened her eyes and waved him off. "Don't start that monkey ball shit. I don't wanna hear you preaching like Farrakhan today. I just wanna enjoy my high without you ruining it. Damn, can I do that?"

He collected the paraphernalia off of the table. "You know what, Momma, I love you. I can't stop you from doing things that kill you, but what I can do is not allow you to do them in my house, and in front of me. I love you too much to watch you die before me." He grabbed her by the arm picking her up.

She swung at him. "Boy, let me go. I ain't got time for yo shit today."

He went into his pocket and gave her a bundle of money. I didn't know how much exactly, but it looked like a lot, considering the top bill was a hundred-dollar one. I figured the majority of the knot had to be. "Momma, I want you out of my house. I don't care where you go, or what you do, but I want you out of here, now!" He pulled her toward the door.

She looked like she had lost her fight. The only thing she kept on staring at was the bundle of money now in her hands. She gave me a look that said she had hit the jackpot.

After he closed the door, he laid his back against it and lowered his head. I walked over to him. "Hey, you need a hug or something?" In response, he opened his arms, and I walked into them.

Ghost

Chapter 5
Lil' Momma

"Aiight, Lil' Momma. Now these niggas we finna hit right here got a Lil' clout in the hood, which means that we can't allow no mistakes. They got plenty niggas that's pledging their loyalties to them, and they the ones that give out rank in the Crip gang. So, if we were to make any mistakes and one of them was able to identify us, we'd have a whole bunch of mafuckas at our head. And you already know how small L.A. is. It wouldn't be long before one or the both of us was bodied." J.T. passed me the blunt. "The reason why I'm telling you this shit is so you can always know the level of danger you stepping into. This shit ain't a game. Anytime you put on that mask, you gotta be ready to play for keeps. This mask mean murder! You got that?"

I took the blunt from him, with my eyes wide open. I was trying my best to process everything he was saying. I didn't wanna miss nothing, and the fact that he was saying our lives could depend on what steps we took, I knew it was crucial that I didn't miss a word of what he was putting down. "Yeah, I got you, baby."

He reached over and trailed his thumb across my lips. "I know the average mafucka will look at you and think because you a female and all small and shit, that you ain't a threat, but I know you got that killer shit in you. Life been fucking you over since. You supposed to hate this world just like I do." He frowned. "We gotta eat by any means, and I don't trust no nigga out here more than I do you. That nigga, Red, was my last homeboy. Now I'm through fucking wit niggas. Every time I see a nigga now, all I see is prey, and that's how I want you to get. I need that beast to come out of right here." He poked me in the chest.

"Well, baby, I'm down for you in every way, just lead and I'm gon' follow." I bit into my bottom lip.

He nodded, went under the seat and came up with a .380 with a beam on top of it. It had a pearl handle, with an extended clip. "This you right here. You cock that mafucka like this, and that puts one in the chamber." He popped out the clip.

"You got seventeen shots in here, because this an extended clip. Whenever you buss, you make that shit count. Fuck aiming for the body, you fuck a nigga over by knocking his head off. Splatter his shit. If you feel like you can't hit that head, then you make sure you aim at the upper body. In this region." He touched my heart, and in the middle of my chest. "Anytime you buss, you keep your eyes wide open just like I taught you. And fuck holding the gun sideways, you hold that mafucka up like it's supposed to be held. That movie shit ain't real. Most of these guns don't be made right, so it'll make it difficult to aim. So, you gotta do your part by getting the best shot you can, because at the end of the day, it's all about fucking over that target."

He rubbed my chin and once again, his thumb ran across my bottom lip. I watched him put two .44 Desert Eagles on his lap, cocking one first and then the other one. The clips in them were so long, they looked like table legs. He frowned and looked out of the window toward the house we were parked two garages down from. We were in an abandoned garage, in the back alleyway. The garage had a broken window on the side of it that allowed us to look out.

"Alright, boo, just follow my lead."

We walked into the backyard, and there was a pitbull chained to the fence. It was so fat, it didn't even bother barking at us when we walked past it. It simply yawned, and closed its eyes.

J.T. walked to the back door and beat on it. He had his ski mask rolled up on his head like it was a regular cap. Mine was the same way. He beat on the door again, this time a little harder.

"Say Cuz, who the fuck out there beating on the door?" said a voice on the other side. It sounded like a male.

"Yo, this T-Money. I come to get some of that dog food, my nigga," J.T. lied, making sure the silencers on his gun were properly screwed in.

I heard what seemed like a two by four being lifted off of the door, and then it slowly began to open. As soon as it did, *VOMP! VOMP! VOMP!* J.T. shot the fat man three times in the face, splattering his tomato all over the side of the door frame.

The man shook for a few seconds, tried to cover his face and then fell forward, with his face bouncing off of the ground. We rolled down our masks and then, J.T. stepped on the dead man's back to get into the house and I followed his same path.

I felt some type of way at first by stepping on a man that had been killed, but then I remembered him telling me that my heart had to be cold, so in that moment I hated the man we'd just killed and even more, I was happy he was dead.

I followed J.T. into the house, and right at the bottom of the steps was another man who had a shotgun in his hand. As soon as he saw us, he looked like he was getting ready to buss. J.T. saw him and *VOMP! VOMP!* He shot and hit the man in the middle of the forehead. The bullet ripped through his forehead and left a hole so big, his blood started oozing out of it before he even hit the ground.

We ran down the stairs with guns pointed. "Alright, you bitch ass niggas, lay it the fuck down. Y'all already know what time it is!" J.T. growled, as the men gathered around a round table with five kilos of dope on top of it, gave him a look showing we'd caught them completely off guard.

One older man with gray cornrows in his head slammed his hand on the table. "Now, how the fuck this happen, Cuz? How the fuck is these niggas in my shit right now, partna?" He looked around the room with obvious anger.

Besides him, there were five other men. Three were sitting around the table with masks over their faces, I imagined to shield them from inhaling the dope they were bagging up. And then there were two men walking around with shotguns. These were the two men J.T. and I had our guns aimed at.

"Fuck nigga, you ain't got time to be asking no questions. Take all of that dope and put it in this bag right here," J.T. said, pulling a garbage bag out of his drawers and popping it so it straightened out. He tossed it to the older man at the table. "Put my shit in there."

The older man grabbed the bag, and mugged J.T. like he wanted to kill him. He looked at all of the dope on the table, and shook his head. "Nawl, fuck this. Say, homie, I can't go out like this, man. I ain't about to have you come into my spot and take my shit away. That's five bricks of pure Peruvian Flake, you gotta leave me with something."

"First of all, you bitch ass niggas drop them shotguns and kick 'em over here!" J.T. raised the Desert Eagles and his eyes got low.

Very slowly, the two men lowered the shotguns to the basement floor. Then, they kicked them over, so they landed by my foot. I didn't know if he wanted me to pick them up, or leave them where they were, so I didn't do anything.

"Aiight, all you niggas get on the floor. On yo muthafucking stomachs, now!" he hollered so loud my ears rang.

56

One by one, they dropped to the floor, scooting their chairs away from the table before falling on their faces. All dropped, but the older man with the gray cornrows.

"Watch these niggas, shawty," J.T. said, pointing down at the men on the ground. Then he walked over to the older man and smacked him across the face with the pistol so hard, it split his face. He put the gun to his forehead, and *Vomp!* I saw a ball of fire shoot from his gun, and then the older man's head exploded, sending blood flying everywhere.

He flew backward and landed twisted up on the ground, right next to the men I was holding at gunpoint.

"You niggas think this a muthafucking game? Huh? Niggas, this ski mask business!" He leaned down and bussed another dude in the back of the head, splattering him all over my shoes. The other men started to get up from fear of being assassinated next.

"Please, bro! Don't kill me!" a skinny dude begged, with his hands in the air. "I got the combination to the safe. That's my father. I'll tell you everything," he promised.

J.T. grabbed him by the neck and flung him against the wall. He slammed into it with his back, making a loud smacking sound before he fell to the floor, and looked to be out cold. "The rest of you niggas strip! Take off all of that jewelry, and throw yo money in a pile. If I search any one of you and you got so much as a dust mite on you, I'm bodying that ass."

They started throwing their watches and jewelry in a pile, right next to knots and knots of money. I could not believe they were holding like that, because most of them looked like bums. They looked like your average, run-of-the-mill street hustlers, working for somebody else. So, I was impressed, to say the least.

I watched J.T. take the five bricks from the table and throw them in the black plastic bag. He slid it over to me and I started to put all of the men's watches, money, and jewelry inside of it as well.

"This better be everything y'all got," J.T. said, bending over and searching them one by one.

Stepping back, I raised my head to survey the area. I wanted to make sure that everything was on point.

Boom! Boom! Boom! I bussed six times and hit the man J.T. had thrown against the wall, all in his neck and face. It looked like somebody had attacked him with a paintball gun, as he slid down the wall into a puddle of blood. The gun he had aimed at J.T. dropped out of his hand after I popped him the first time.

J.T. turned around and looked at his dead body, and then over at me. He stood up, and emptied his guns into the remaining men. *Vomp! Vomp! Vomp! Vomp! Vomp!*

"Aaaaah, you bitch ass niggas trying to snake meeee!" He picked up the shotguns and emptied them into the men as well, and then threw them in the bag with the rest of the merchandise. "Let's go!"

"You saved my life, baby! My baby girl saved my muthafucking life. Damn, I can't believe I was slipping like that!" he said and slammed his hands against the steering wheel.

We had already stopped back at home and dropped all of the stuff off we'd gotten from the lick. Now we were rolling around the streets of L.A. and I was trying my best to not freak out after killing my first person. It was one thing to watch somebody else kill something. But, when you did the shit yourself, it brought on a whole new emotion.

"Baby, it's gon' be okay. That's what I was there for. I was supposed to have yo back. That's what you taught me. So, the fact that I did, all you're supposed to be is proud, and know that your baby girl listened to everything you say. Know that you puttin' it down the way you supposed to be," I said, reaching over and squeezing his thigh.

He adjusted himself in the driver's seat. I could tell he was still bothered being caught slipping. "Nawl, baby, it ain't that I'm not proud of you. It's just that I was on some bullshit, and I wasn't supposed to be. I ain't have no reason to throw that nigga against the wall without searching him. Then, I turned my back on him, and just completely underestimated him on all levels. That ain't my character. Had I been with anybody else, I would have been bodied. I can't see no other nigga I fucked with, catching that mistake the way you did. I feel like fucking yo brains out right now. Matter fact..." He whipped the car over two lanes, and then parked it in front of a Blockbuster video store.

J.T. leaned my seat all the way back, and pulled my Fendi skirt up on my hips, exposing my raspberry-colored Chanel thong. I felt him pull them to the side and then, he sucked my pussy lips into his mouth like he was eating sushi, before sliding his tongue through my crease.

"Baby, what are you doing?" I asked as I watched a family of white people walk into the store, thankful they were paying our car no mind.

"I want you to come all over my tongue. This my way of bowing down to yo gangsta. You saved my life, now come for me, Lil' Momma." He opened my pussy lips with his fingers, and then I felt him slide at least three fingers into my hole.

He started fucking them into me so fast, I felt like I couldn't breathe. He had his lips wrapped around my pearl, flicking his tongue back and forth, making loud ass slurping noises that drove me crazy.

"Unnn-unnn, unnn-shit. J.T., you eating that shit, baby! You got me going crazy, daddy! You got me going fucking crazy."

I held my thighs open wider for him. I didn't care that people were walking past the car now, and one heavyset female pushing a stroller looked in and saw what we were doing. That just made me open my thighs wider.

"Come for me, Lil' Momma! Come in my mouth. You deserve it, baby."

I felt him nipping on my clit with his teeth and that was all I could take. I grabbed his head and forced his face all into my pussy. I mean, I was rough with him, opening my legs as far as they could go. "Ahhhhhh-shiiiit! Babeeeeee!" I screamed, coming harder than I ever had before. I started humping into his mouth, and rocking back and forth.

He ran about three of his fingers in and out of me at full speed and they were bussing me open. My pussy started skeeting. I could hear my noisy juices squishing as his fingers flew in and out. "Yeah, that's my girl. That's my baby right there. Yeah, I love this shit," he said, rubbing his thumb across my clit in a circular motion, which had me bucking up into him. "Damn, look at all this juice."

He slurped all the shit up and it made me shiver. "When we get home tonight, I'mma dick you down better than ever. I gotta keep you cherished, because you mean the world to me, Lil' Momma."

Chapter 6
Jennifer

I was starting to feel a little better after getting a couple nights' rest. I finally felt hungry, like when I actually put something on my stomach, I was gon' be able to keep it down.

So, I fixed a ham and cheese sandwich, with mustard and plenty mayo. I cut it diagonally like I had been doing ever since I was a kid. Grabbing a fun-sized bag of Doritos, and a Hawaiian Punch, I started to throw down, eating like I ain't have no home training. I ate the sandwich so fast, I don't even think I got the chance to really taste it.

I was in the middle of making the second sandwich when Lil' Momma and J.T. came in the house, laughing at the top of their lungs. J.T. came past me and gave me a brief hug, then went into the back of the house, and closed the bathroom door. Lil' Momma walked up to me and was about to give me a hug, but then stopped and looked me up and down.

I froze, like I had done something wrong. The first thought that came to my head was, maybe she was feeling some type of way, because I was in her man's house with some Daisy Dukes on. In fact, I had not even realized I had them on until that moment. "What?" I asked, looking at her nervously, suddenly feeling naked. I tried to cover myself and must have looked like a damn fool.

"Jennifer, I kilt a nigga today and I'm geeked. I knocked his shit all against the wall." She jumped a little bit with her eyes so wide, it looked like she'd been smoking crack. But, I knew better than that. My cousin rarely fucked with any type of drugs, and crack definitely wasn't an option.

"Wait a minute, what happened?" I asked, wanting her to dish all of the tea. I was excited to know what had taken place, and how she felt to have actually killed somebody.

She grabbed me by the hand and took me into an empty bedroom. "Me and J.T. had to take care of some business that I won't get to much into, but during that business move, some nigga got the ups on him, and before he could kill my man, I splashed his ass. I shot him six times all in this region," she said, pointing to my head and neck area. "Fuck, I'm geeked!"

I put my hand on her back and rubbed it. I knew that she was floating on air and I didn't want to bring her off of her high, but at the same time I knew how my little cousin was. She would bottle things up that bothered her, and then she would behave in the craziest of ways, kinda like she was doing at that moment.

"Lil' Momma, you know I got rid of Bobby and Liz. At first, I was happy about the whole ordeal, but then slight traces of remorse started to set in. It caused me to have nightmares and I even got depressed. I felt like I had done something very wrong, and I would never be forgiven for it. Are you sure you're okay all across the board?"

She waved her hand through the air as if to dismiss the whole notion. "Look, I don't give a fuck no more. Them streets out there hate me, and they hate you. J.T. is the only mafucka trying to shield us in any way. So, I'm gon' follow his lead. He kills and I'll kill. If he tells me to kill, I'm gon' kill with no hesitation. I've never felt more powerful in my whole life." She curled her upper lip, and her eyes got evil. "Ever since I was a little kid, all people have ever done was push me around, and take advantage of me. Nobody has ever stood up for me, ever! I've been killed a thousand times over. Every time my mother's husband entered my body, he killed me. Every time my mother knew it was happening and didn't do anything about it, she killed me. Every time a man cheated on me, I died. Every punch, slap, push, and kick I received at the hands of another person, caused me pain and took my life. Well, I'm tired of being the only one that dies. I'm ready to kill some shit!"

I had tears in my eyes as I listened to her talk. The feeling of her pains were mutual for me. I hurt in the same ways she did, and I understood where she was coming from. I wanted to say so much to her, but I couldn't find the words. I simply pulled her into my arms and hugged her tightly.

J.T. walked into the room and snatched her up, making her wrap her legs around him. He crashed into the wall with her and they made out like they were trying to eat each other up. He pulled her shirt over her head, and then ripped her bra from her body. Her A-cup titties spilled out, with huge nipples that stood up like pacifiers. He lowered his head and sucked on one so loud, a spark went right to my clit. I closed my legs together and squeezed them.

"Oooh-shit, baby. You know I love it when you suck all hard on my nipples," Lil' Momma moaned. She threw her head back while he sucked on first one, and then the other.

J.T. groaned as he pulled Lil' Momma's Fendi skirt all the way around her waist, exposing her naked pussy, and then dropped his Tom Ford denim shorts, along with his boxers.

When I saw his dick sticking out of his waist as big as a caveman's club, both of my nipples got hard, and I felt my heartbeat speed up. His dick head looked like the Arby's logo.

He slammed her into the wall again and held her up against it, before taking his huge dick head and stuffing it past her sex lips. She tightened her arms around his neck and closed her eyes.

"Oh, shit! Baby, there you go again. There you go, all in my fuckin' stomach!" she screamed as he bounced her up and down on his brown cucumber.

My pussy was dripping wet. I felt that shit running all down my inner thighs, and my coochie was jumping. I squeezed my thighs together, and moaned deep within my throat. I couldn't take my eyes away from his dick going in and out of her. Every time he would pull out, her lips looked like they were trying to trap him back inside. Then when he slammed her ass down on it, his balls would smack against her wet pussy and it made a sound that was driving me crazy.

Before I could even stop myself, my hand went into my panties and I slid my fingers over my naked pussy lips. I moaned, watching his dick punish her. It wasn't long before I was brazenly fingering myself with three fingers, watching them go at it like barbarians.

J.T. fell to the floor with her and pushed her into a ball. Both her knees were to her chest with him lining his big dick up to her hole. They were laying sideways to me, so I could see her pussy buss open once he pushed her knees to her chest. "I'm finna kill this shit, Lil' Momma. I'm about to show you what it do when I love yo ass." He cocked all the way back, and rammed his dick forward and deep into her.

She yelped, and started moaning so loud, I thought the people outside would hear her. "Fuck me, J.T. Fuck me, daddy! Harder baby, harderrrr!" she screamed.

His ass was a blur as he smashed into her again and again. It sounded like somebody was in the room, constantly clapping their hands. I could even hear the sounds of his dick sliding in and out of her pussy juices.

I was on my knees, with my fingers running in and out of me at a hundred miles an hour, it seemed. I couldn't take my eyes off of his dick. I saw the way it was punishing her lil' pussy and started imagining what my cousin was feeling at that moment.

It was turning me on so bad, I wanted to go over there and ask her if I could fuck her man, if only for a few minutes. I imagined him rolling me into a ball and fucking me hard, while he choked me a little bit. He would be rough with me, breaking me in the right way. Sucking on my nipples as hard as he did hers. Then, I would make him fuck me from the back, while he spanked me and pulled my hair.

I felt myself coming, and I was trying to do everything I could not to scream. I had pulled my Daisy Dukes down a little bit to give me room to do my thing, so my naked pussy was exposed. My fingers flew in and out of me, and I zoomed in on his big dick. The shakes started and the next thing I knew, I had fallen on my back, coming super hard while I fucked up onto my fingers.

As soon as I came, I looked over at J.T. and he and I made eye contact. He smiled and then pulled his dick all the way out of Lil' Momma, rubbed it around her pussy, licked his lips, then slid back into her. All the while, his eyes trailed down to my naked pussy.

Later that night, I found myself up watching a Tyler Perry movie on Netflix. Well, I wasn't actually watching it, it was more like it was watching me, as I tried to get ahold of my thoughts. I needed to figure out what I was going to do with my life, now that Bobby was dead. I was completely lost, and had no idea what I even wanted out of life. He had me so controlled, I never found myself thinking past the things that he wanted and expected of me. I felt like a slave with had no freedom date. I felt like my world revolved around him and his demands.

About an hour after I had been sitting there lost in thought, J.T. knocked on the guest room door before sticking his head in. "I saw the light from the TV in here shining from under the door. I thought you was in here sleep with it on again, and I was gon' turn it off."

I sat up in the bed, and shook my head. "Nawl, I can't sleep for some reason." I shuffled, feeling a little uneasy in the big bed. I think I felt a little shy because I had seen what he was working with in his pants, and I knew he'd seen my kitty too.

He stepped all the way in the room with his shirt off. I had never paid attention to how ripped up he really was, but this time I did, and I was impressed. His abs were popping. It looked like all he did all day was sit-ups and crunches. His chest was well defined and for a man, he had nice-sized nipples that reminded me of mini chocolate drops.

He was already handsome, and though I was crazy about tattoos, he had only one. A tear drop right in the corner of his left eye and closer to his cheek, made him look even more sexy to me. I began feeling guilty as hell, because I knew he was my cousin's man, and they had a strong bond. I tried to shut off those womanly desires in me that screamed out for his fine ass. And, the fact that he had rescued me from my impossible situation didn't help matters either.

He climbed onto the bed, and wrapped me in his arms. "Well, lucky for you, I can't sleep either. I got a whole lot of shit on my mind, and it's making it hard for me. So, I'll tell you what, if you tell me what's on your mind, I'll tell you what's on mine." He held me a little tighter, and I could feel his chest muscles up against my shoulder, that immediately got me wet.

"I guess I just feel lost," I said, squeezing my thighs together. I already felt the fire beginning deep within my womb and I was trying to extinguish it, before it turned into a wildfire. "You know, when I was with Bobby, he never let me do anything, or go anywhere, so I lost sight of what freedom is. I started to basically live in his prison and by doing so, it caused me to lose sight of myself."

J.T. kissed me on the forehead and started rubbing my shoulder. The smell of his cologne went up my nose and seemed to pull on my nipples, until they were as hard as pebbles. I hoped he didn't notice them, because I was only wearing a very sheer, red nightgown. After telling Lil' Momma I needed something to wear to bed, she'd given it to me, and I had slept in it ever since.

"Go ahead, I want you to get it all out," he said, before rubbing his cheek against my own.

I shivered. "I guess what I'm saying is that I need to find my dreams. I need to find the part of me that wants to be something in life, because right now I am completely lost, and I don't feel worthy of anything other than pain. Bobby was the one that supplied everything for me. It's been that way ever since I was a little girl. Now that I have to step out on my own, I feel so scared, lost, and alone. I don't know what to do, and I guess I'm starting to freak out some." I lowered my head onto his chest and unconsciously started rubbing his abs. They felt hard and hot, like if you warmed up an ice tray, and rubbed up and down the ripples on the bottom of it.

"First of all, Jennifer, you are very much worthy, because you are a queen, no matter what Bobby told you. You didn't need him then, and you don't need him now. You don't need nobody other than you." He grabbed my chin and made me look up at him. "Now, don't get me wrong, because I got you and I'm gon' hold you down better than any other nigga ever has. I'm gon' be that loyalty in your life. Me and Lil' Momma. We gon' be one family, and we gon' make shit happen together, so all you gotta do is decide what you want to do with your life, and where you wanna go, then we gon' all make sure you able to make it happen. We all gotta be here for one another, because this world hates us, Jennifer, and if we sit back and just allow life to happen, we gon' always wind up being the prey instead of the predators. Because you can only be one or the other. There is no in-between."

I felt him running his fingers through my hair and it felt very comforting. "So, what do you suppose I do, then?" I asked, turning over some so I could look into his eyes.

"That all depends on where you want to go in life. You have to get your goals and dreams in check. Only then will you be able feel better about yourself, because you'll know where you're headed."

He made me lay my head back on his chest. My ear landed right over his heart. I could hear it beating, and it sounded like it was working overtime. I wondered if maybe he was just as nervous as I was. I wished Lil' Momma had been in the next room, because that would have prevented me from having so many erotic thoughts and feelings about him. I knew I would never purposely do anything to hurt her, and I was sure that J.T. wouldn't have either.

"Okay then, let's take you for instance, J.T. What are your goals, and what do you want to do in life?"

He was silent for a long time. All that could be heard was the sound of the fan blowing on us from the dresser top. I felt him readjust himself, and then he took a deep breath and blew it out. "I wanna get out of L.A. and move to New York, where I could start my own movie production company. I got all of these ideas in my head for a movie and about a year ago, I sent a movie script off to a producer out there and he was all over it. The name of the script was *Raised As A Goon* and he said it was hot. He sent me a contract in the mail and everything, but a week later, I wound up getting locked up and the police tore the crib up. I ain't been able to find the contract, or the dude's information since then. But, while I was in there, I did write parts one, two, and three to the book, and I just sent that off to this major nigga down in Georgia that got his own publishing company. I'm just waiting to hear back from him."

"Dang, you wrote three books though?" I asked, amazed. Hell, I didn't even know he liked to write.

"Yeah, but it's more like eighteen total. Sometimes the demons of all the mafuckas I done kilt be haunting me, and the only thing I can do is write about 'em. I see shit so clear. But, one day, I just wanna have my books published, and film my movies. I feel like everybody should be able to see this shit that goes on in my head. I'm tired of being alone wit it."

Damn, he was blowing my mind. I guess everybody had a little loneliness and sadness at the root. It took for you to really dive into a person, before you got the chance to see what was really deep within them.

Here it was I thought J.T. was this savage of a man with no dreams and no goals, other than surviving in the streets. But, come to find out, he saw beyond L.A., clear across the country, all the way to New York City.

"I wanna put my mother in a rehab too, 'cuz I'm tired of seeing her kill herself with that poison. I been watching her do that shit all my life, and I'm tired of seeing her hurting the way she is. I looked up some real good celebrity rehab centers that go all out to rehabilitate drug addicts, and I want to send her to one. It's just gon' cost me damn near two hundred G's to do it. So, I gotta get that." He sighed. "But, enough about me. Let's talk about what you did earlier, because you know I saw you three fingers deep all in that lil' red thang down there, right?" he said, putting his face into the crook of my neck, planting a butterfly kiss on it.

I must have blushed as red as a strawberry. He completely caught me off guard with that one. So much so, I didn't even know what to say. I wanted to get up and run out of the room. "What you say, J.T.?" I asked stupidly.

He laughed and kissed my neck again. "Look, it ain't something that gotta be blown out of proportion. I just wanted you to know that I peeped you."

Chapter 7
Lil' Momma

"Lil' Momma, I ain't even gon' lie to you. I feel weird as hell allowing him to take us here and spend all this money on us. I mean, he the only one trying to step up to the plate for the both of us. Don't you feel just a little bit self-conscious?" Jennifer whispered into my ear as we pulled up on Rodeo Drive.

She had her arm around my shoulder and it was already hot and humid. I mean, I loved my cousin, but us being so close together was causing me to sweat a little bit. I politely moved her arm from around my shoulder and kissed her on the cheek.

I had looked behind me to see where J.T. was, and I saw him sitting in the driver's seat of his cherry-red Lexus, counting a stack of hundreds. That made my nipples hard. It was nothing like seeing your man count stacks of hundreds. That shit just made a girl feel all secure and whatnot. "Look, Jenn, we're two beautiful women who ain't really got shit just yet. And we have a man in our lives that's trying to make sure we're straight as much as possible. This nigga got bundles of cash, and whenever it gets low, all we gon' do is go lay some shit down, and get more. We ain't hurting him, and he's helping us. Why should I feel self-conscious when I just blew a nigga's head off for him, just so we could get that money?"

She lowered her head. "I know, but that's you. He's supposed to take care of you because you're his woman, I'm not thought. I feel like he's done enough for me already, and this is just pushing things over the top."

I paused to see where J.T. was again, and saw that he was just starting to get out of the car. I grabbed Jennifer's hands.

"Look, Cuz, if a nigga doing for me, he gotta do for you as well. Ain't no way in hell I'm about to go shopping on

Rodeo Drive, and you sit at home wearing that bullshit you call clothes. You ain't got no crib, no job, or means of supporting yourself right now, so it's my job to make sure that when I'm straight, you're straight. So, just chill and let him take care of us, because ain't nobody else out here trying to do it."

J.T. came and slid his arms over our shoulders. "Look, I want you ladies to do ya thing. Everything is on me today. Y'all been through enough, and it's time to just fall back and be spoiled. You understand that?" he asked, kissing my cheek and then Jennifer's. She looked over at me nervously, and I nodded my head.

"Yeah, baby, show us how daddy ball."

I stepped into the full-length mirror, after sliding on the Elie Saab mini dress priced at twenty-five hundred dollars. Turning in a circle, I loved the way it conformed to my body. I felt feminine as ever. The dress hugged my ass so much, it made it poke way out, then it conformed to my hips and all the way up to my small titties. I took it off and put it in a pile with the rest of the dresses I had accumulated.

Jennifer stood in front of the mirror in a purple and black Roberto Cavalli dress that made her look so sexy, I got jealous I had not seen it first. I mean, she looked super fine. The dress hugged her body like a second skin. I could even see her nipples poking through it.

"Damn, Cuz, you look bad as hell. You make me wanna hit that shit from the back," I joked and smacked her on her juicy ass.

It jiggled for a brief second. She reached her hand down and covered it protectively. "Ouch, girl. You betta stop that shit." She pulled my arm and then smacked me on mine.

I felt a crazy spark shoot through me. And instead of me covering my ass cheeks protectively like she did, I poked my butt out and closed my eyes. "Gon' 'head, and go for what you know," I half-joked. I say half because had she started to spank me in that dressing room, even though she was my cousin, I would have let her and not felt no type of way about it. I loved having my lil' ass spanked, especially when it was poking out the way like it was. J.T. had turned me out to spankings a long time ago and I was hooked.

Jennifer started laughing. "You so damn silly." She patted my booty for a few seconds, and then rubbed it. "You lucky you and J.T. being so nice to me, or else I would spank yo lil' butt until you start crying. "

I felt another shiver go through me as she turned around in the mirror again. The thought of me getting my ass spanked until I cried drove me crazy. I had to put my mind on something else.

"How do you think I look in this dress and I want you to be honest to?" she asked, popping back on her legs and looking over her shoulder.

"Girl, you killing that dress. It got yo ass sitting up right. You definitely doing Roberto Cavalli some justice. That's just me keeping it real," I said, eyeing her big booty, impressed.

We changed into a few more outfits. I had to step my Prada game up some, after getting right with Dolce and Gabbana. I didn't like their politics, but their clothes had me looking super right. Jennifer tried to stop at two outfits, but I made sure she got about seven, which was the same number I had.

After that, we got our shoe game up to par, and a few handbags. The whole time, J.T. sat in the front of the store under the air conditioner, talking on his cell phone. It looked like he was arguing with somebody. I would try to feel him out later on, at that moment I just wanted me and my cousin to enjoy our pampering day.

I walked over to him to tell him we were done shopping and we needed him to come and pay for it. But, before I could get that far, he handed me a knot of money so thick, it looked like a folded dictionary. I grabbed it with two hands. Jennifer's eyes were open so wide, I could see the pink surrounding them. She looked like she was super amazed. I smiled like a boss and walked past her with my eyes closed. I was feeling good, until I bumped into this skinny white girl, who dropped her phone.

She had the nerve to roll her eyes at me, and throw her blonde extensions over her shoulder. "Excuse you, sistah girl, but can you watch where you going? You're not in the hood, you know." She leaned down to pick her phone up, and I almost kicked her in the face. Her and that little ugly ass dog she had in her purse. It looked like something a shark had thrown up.

I knelt down with her. "Excuse you, bitch, but what did you just say to me?" I asked, with my forehead damn near touching hers.

I was ready to whoop that bitch in the store. I didn't give a fuck what my consequences would have been. She grabbed her phone, and took a step back. "Oh my God. Like, am I supposed to be scared or what? Because I am so not." She rolled her eyes. "It's a little hard to do a drive-by in here, sistah girl. So, why don't you just get out of my way, and let me finish my shopping." She sounded like a spoiled rich bitch, drawing out every word, making it sound longer than it actually was.

I almost threw the bundle of money in her face, because I wanted to do something very petty to piss her off. She tried to walk around me, but I blocked her path. "Look, bitch, you don't even know me like that and I'd appreciate it if you didn't act like you did. I hope you don't think you better than me, just because yo lil' pink ass walking around wit that lil' ugly ass dog."

She gasped like she was offended. "Oh my God. No, you didn't. For your information, Jupiter probably costs more than it took for your parents to raise you in the hood. So, if I was you, I'd just shut up or whatever, because you don't even know what you're talking about."

"Uh, is there a problem here?" a taller white girl said with an Alexander McQueen shift suit on that made her look like a model. I could tell she worked there because she had a tag on her top with her name.

"Yeah, there's most definitely a problem here, because this black chick is like, begging me for quarters and that's not cool. She's totally ruining my shopping experience and I would like to see her removed from the store before I take my business elsewhere."

"Asking you for quarters? Bitch, are you serious right now, or have you lost yo rabid ass mind?" I yelled, ready to snap the fuck out.

Jennifer stepped in front of me, just as I was about to punch this punk bitch. "Hey, we didn't ask her for anything. We were about to pay for our things, when my cousin made a mistake and bumped into her, causing her to drop her phone. After she dropped her phone, she said some pretty mean things, and my cousin is just reacting to them in a defensive way. All we'd like to do is pay for our things and go," she said, wrapping her arm around my shoulder.

I threw it off. "Nawl, fuck that. Why don't you kick this bitch out the store for making all of these prejudiced and stereotypical statements? She seriously has a problem with people of color, and that's sad."

The sales girl looked from us to the blonde bitch, and bit into her bottom lip. "Hey, why don't you guys just pay for your things and then everybody goes their separate ways? There shouldn't be any further problems after that, right?" she asked, looking to us.

Now, I was feeling like this bitch was taking the white girl's side. I felt my temper getting red-hot, so much so, my vision was getting cloudy. I imagined myself shooting the blonde bitch in the face and stomping her head. Then, I would knock the sales girl's brains out, and play soccer with her shit.

"Yeah, that'll be cool. We'll just pay for our things and get lost," Jennifer said, walking to the counter and bumping the shit out of the white girl, so hard that her dog yelped.

The blonde girl wrapped her hands around him protectively, and ran into one of the aisles. "You guys are mean! I hate you!" she hollered, and a security guard walked over to her and they began to talk.

I shrugged my shoulders. I walked to the front of the store, and paid for our things. A part of me wanted to say fuck buying anything from that store, after the way the sales girl looked at us, but I wanted that gear J.T. had snatched up for us. I felt like I deserved it, and I wasn't about to let no stuck-up, privileged white snob take that away from me.

***

I laid on my stomach while this big ass Brazilian dude massaged my back so firmly, I wanted to marry his ass. He smelled a little weird for my taste, but I just chalked that up to a culture clash. Maybe his breed of women thought he smelled good, but I definitely did not. That ain't stop me from falling deep into a zone over his massage though.

"Juu like thee massage, ma'am, or would juu like me to go harder?" he asked, rolling his thumbs around in my lower back.

I spread my legs because I wanted him to smell how wet he had me. I was ass naked under that sheet, and I felt like a nigga. Before I left there, I was gon' make him give me a happy ending. "Nawl, that feels good, Paco. Just go down as far as you can and don't forget to get my glutes. I need the kinks worked out of them," I purred and laid my head back into the little hole that accommodated my face.

"Okay, yes no problemo," he said as I felt his big hands trail down to my cheeks, before rolling them around like dough. I even felt him open them up and then a constant, cool breeze blew right on my hole.

I moaned and popped my thighs apart, because it was feeling so damn good. "Yeah, Paco, just like that, baby." I looked over my shoulder and saw he had his face all in between my goodies, just sniffing me up. That shit turned me all the way on, especially when I felt something wet touch my clitoris. I arched my back, and damn near did the splits.

"Juu want a happy ending, Mamita? It cost no extra, and it be my pleasure to do for juu," he said, and once again I felt the cool air on my asshole. He had spread my cheeks again, leaving me wide open.

I tried to imagine what Jennifer was doing in the other room during her Gold Package Spa treatment. I knew she had to be experiencing the same treatment, because before we went into our rooms, J.T. had told us to enjoy ourselves, and to get a happy ending. He said he planned on getting him one from the Brazilian broad that led him away by the hand. She had more ass than a donkey. I had watched her ass jiggle and shake in the little green thong. I had been tempted to go in the room with them, because I thought she was gon' steal my man.

I didn't care if it was purely physical. But, she was so fine, I found myself getting intimidated. I hoped he would not get her number, because I could not compete with that bitch. At least, I didn't think so.

"Yeah, Paco, make yo Lil' Mami feel good, Papi. I need it," I said, getting on all fours.

He grabbed me by the waist, pushed my thighs apart, took two fingers and spread my pussy lips way apart. I could feel the cool breeze going up my hole, right before his lips sucked on my pearl roughly.

"Unnnn-uh shit, Paco. Suck me, Papi. Make me love it." I moaned and spread my ass cheeks all the way apart. They were spread so far, I was hurting myself.

He stuck his face in between them, and started to slurp all over my sex, and lick his tongue up and down my ass crack. He began making a whole lot of loud noises, and I was starting to get off just on them alone. When he slapped my ass, I damn near came everywhere. "Unnn-shit!"

He slapped it again, and then started eating me for all I was worth. I stuck my hand between my legs, playing with my clitoris. My juices poured in between my fingers, and only made me mash my clitoris harder. "Smack it again, Paco. Smack my lil' ass, please!" I hollered.

He smacked me on the ass again, and spread my ass cheeks. I felt his thumb enter my tight hole, and that was all I needed to come. My body started shaking, and I got to making noises I didn't even know I knew how to make. He kept on sucking and slurping, until I fell on my stomach, shaking like I was having a horrible seizure.

***

As we rolled back in the car, I looked into the backseat at Jennifer. Her ass was glowing. She looked like she'd had a thousand spa days in a row. I mean, she was beaming. "Damn, girl, I see you back there, looking all refreshed and shit. You care to dish the tea?" I teased, and she turned red.

"Huh?" she said, dumbfounded, but I could see the guilt written all over her face.

"Huh, my ass. I know you was all in South America with that fine ass nigga you had. Now say you wasn't," I dared.

She smiled and lowered her head. "Well, I mean, let's just say that I enjoyed my massage and I really can't complain." She smiled again. "Thank you, J.T., you're the best."

He nodded and pushed in the car lighter, preparing to light a big blunt that looked like a brown baby leg. "As long as you enjoyed yourself, that's all that matters to me. I already know this one over here did, so don't let her make you feel all guilty and shit." He lit the blunt and a thick cloud of smoke invaded the car. Just from inhaling the second-hand smoke, I started to cough. That shit smelled stronger than the Incredible Hulk.

"Guilty? I ain't trying to make her feel guilty, because I definitely enjoyed myself. I made Paco put his fine ass face all in my creases. He licked me so good, I asked him if he needed a green card."

They started bussing up laughing. "Yo, I did my thing with Alissa too. She tried her best to swallow me whole, but couldn't quite get there. So, I was cool wit bussing in her pretty face, and making her rub my shit all over her lips and nose. Oh, and the massage was nice too, I think," he said, laughing.

I punched him in the leg. "What you mean, you think? At least, I did get a massage first. He just had me feeling some type of way. I had to come on his tongue, or else I was finna come in there and break that shit up with you and Alissa, because I needed some relief."

"I'm glad you didn't. Everybody had they own room. So, if you ain't take care of business in there, that's yo fault." I grabbed the big blunt from him and pulled on it. I could barely get the smoke in my mouth, before I was choking like I swallowed a fish bone. J.T. hit me on the back and that ain't do no damn good. I wanted to punch his ass because it seemed like that only made my coughs worse. I lowered my window and stuck my head out.

"Damn, girl, you know you got asthma and bronchitis, you can't be smoking that shit he blowing," Jennifer said, rubbing my back.

I had my tongue sticking out of my mouth like a dog in need of water. I should have known better than to just take a blunt from J.T. and start smoking. That fool always managed to find the strongest, most potent weed in California. I was already so high, it felt like my head was floating in front of my body, like it was a balloon or something.

"Jennifer, we gotta get Lil' Momma home so she can lay down. She look like she fucked up," J.T. said, waving his hand in front of my face, before taking his blunt from my hand.

"Yeah, y'all drop me off at home, because I know my people already tripping and shit. I need to lay down for a few hours anyway."

Chapter 8
Jennifer

"Damn, you popped this big ass bowl of popcorn, like we finna be up all night watching movies and shit. Did you at least put some seasoned salt on it?" J.T. asked as he grabbed the big bowl from my hands.

I handed him the hot sauce, and rolled my eyes. "Some people would have the courtesy to say thank you for getting up and handling this task." I put my hand on my hip and looked down at him like I was waiting on something.

He laughed, reached, and pulled me down by my pink wife beater. I landed on the side of him. A little popcorn had fallen out of the bowl. So, when I sat down, I felt my ass crunching some of it. "Nawl, you know I'm kidding. Thank you for taking care of this business. I appreciate you."

I blushed and lowered my head. "You welcome, J.T., dang. You always trying to make people get all mushy and shit."

He wrapped his arm around me as the movie, *Girl's Trip*, started to play. "This shit better be funny too. You got a nigga watching a chick flick, all hugged up. Man, y'all trying to turn me soft," he joked, and dug his hand into the popcorn.

"I ain't never seen it before, but from what they saying, it's supposed to be good. Real funny too, so I guess we gon' see," I said, laying my head on his shoulder.

He kissed me on the forehead and moved my long hair out of the way, exposing the portion of my neck closest to him. He leaned in and kissed it once, and then went in again and sucked on it with his thick lips, making a loud sucking noise.

"You always smell so damn good, Jenn." He kissed me on it again, then wrapped his arm around me and laid back.

My nipples were so hard, they were hurting. Not only that, but my pussy was throbbing worse than I ever remember it throbbing before. I felt my hole juicing up, and I got to moving around uncomfortably on that couch. I could still feel where his lips were on my neck. I felt like I needed to say something, but I couldn't think of anything right off the bat. So, I was silent for about ten minutes, before he grabbed my hand and made me rub his naked abs. Ugh, that shit got me even wetter, because to me, there was nothing like some rock-hard abs on a man.

I mean, don't get me wrong. I liked men with a lil' gut too, but there was just something about abs, especially on a black man that drove me crazy. So, I got to rubbing his shit, and even running my nails across them occasionally.

"Damn, your hands so soft," he said and laid all the way back. He pulled his shorts down a little more so I could see the line that comes before the pubic area. You know, the line that's right under the abs that make bitches open they legs right up? I trailed my fingers along that line, while he closed his eyes. My face kept getting closer and closer to his stomach, until I was actually trailing my lips against it.

I kissed his abs, and then I bit them with my teeth. His skin was hot, and his scent shot up my nose, causing my pearl to peek out of the top of my sex lips.

"Taste me, Jennifer. Stop playing wit my body. We family, baby. So, taste me," he moaned and laid all the way down on the couch.

I slid in between his legs, and pulled his shorts down. He wasn't wearing any boxers. His dick was already at half-mast and looked like a brown garden snake, trying to slither its way to full-length. I grabbed it and stroked it up and down.

I kissed its big head and ran my tongue back and forth across it. He tasted a little salty, and I liked it.

"Come on, Jenn. Stop playing with me, baby. Lace me, and I got you next. I promise." He reached over my shoulder and grabbed a handful of my ass, shaking it, before sliding his fingers through the leg holes of my boy shorts. When I felt his fingers on my hairless yellow pussy, I opened my legs wide.

"Ummm, J.T.," I said as he slid two fingers deep into me.

I had one knee raised on the couch, and the other one was on the floor. My head was in his lap, and my eyes were closed, wishing he would put a hurting on my pussy.

He took my little hand and made me stroke his dick up and down, until it was standing as tall as the Eiffel Tower. Then he grabbed a handful of my hair, and slowly directed me to inhale him, which I did.

As soon as he was in my mouth, I didn't play no games. I got to deep throating him like I was a porn star, and I was trying to build up my fan base. Had somebody recorded me in action, the footage would have gone viral. I got to rubbing his shit all over my face, and lips. Nipping at it with my teeth, then swallowing him whole. And, I was on some gangsta shit too, because I had my hands behind my back on my professional shit.

I knew that nigga was a killer, but he made some noises I knew he'd feel some type of way about, when it was all said and done.

When he got to bucking up off of the couch real fast, I figured he was on his way to coming. His dick got as big as a Star Wars light saber, and fat as a flashlight. I was stroking it so fast, my hand was a blur.

"Arrrrgh-shit, shit, shit!" he groaned, and then his pole was spilling over. I trapped his seed with my lips and started swallowing, like I had been stuck in the desert for a full week and this was my first taste of water. He tasted salty and fruity at the same time.

The next thing I knew, he had me folded up on the couch sucking on my pearl while I cussed his ass out. He had three fingers going in and out of me at full speed. "Give me this shit, Jenn. Come for me, baby. Let me taste that shit. Please, let me taste all of that shit," he begged and trailed his tongue in circles all around my clit.

"Unn-unnna, Unnn-unnna, shit! J.T., you killing me, you killing me, baabbbeeee!" I screamed and started bucking like I was trying to get him off of me.

The more I came, the harder he sucked. Even when my clit got so sensitive that I wanted to punch his ass, I had to fight through it, and that led me to another orgasm.

Then, he carried me to his room, and laid me across the big bed on my stomach. He spread my legs, and knelt between them.

I then felt him open my ass, and he licked all in between my crack. Cleaning up my juices from my crease in the middle.

I laid there with my head on my arms. I questioned if I was betraying Lil' Momma by doing what I was doing. She had said J.T. was our protector. That he was there to make sure we were always taken care of. She had allowed him and the Brazilian girl to do their thing, and she didn't seem as if she had been jealous at all. In fact, she even did her own thing in the other room, she'd confessed. So, as I laid there and felt J.T. kissing all over my ass cheeks, and rolling them in his big hands, I truly wondered if I was betraying my cousin.

"Damn you got a big ass booty, Jenn. I always noticed that shit too. I ain't seen many bad females like you out here in Cali with a perfect ass like that," he said and ran his finger through my crack. I cocked my legs wide open for him. Showing him everything I had to offer. My yellow pussy was popped out, and ready for action. Oozing like a person sleeping and slobbing on they pillow.

"Thank you, J.T. It's yours for tonight. I'm yours for tonight. Whatever you wanna do to me, I'm game."

I felt him climb onto my back, then he ran his big dick head up and down my slit, teasing me until I reached back and guided him into me. His dick slipped into my cave like a hot butter knife slipping into butter. I had to close my eyes really tight as I felt him filling me up more and more.

"Damn, this shit hot. You got some good pussy, girl. I knew you would though." He laid on top of me and sucked on my neck while he slowly went in and out of me. Pulling all the way back before slamming his huge pipe deep into my channel.

I had tears in my eyes already because that shit was feeling so good. That was one reason, and the other one was because, he was the first male that had ever been inside my body I actually cared about and wanted to be there. It just felt awesome. "Umm-umm, J.T. Huhhh, oh shit! I love it, baby! Fuck me just like that! Just like that, baby!" I moaned with tears rolling off my cheeks.

He grabbed my waist and pulled me up so I was on all fours. Slow-stroking me, and crashing into my ass every chance he got. "I would kill this shit, Jennifer. But, you need a man that's gon' make love to this body, because you been through so much. I told you from here on out, I got you. That I'm gon' be the one to protect you against all odds. And, I meant that shit. This my pussy now. I'm gon' keep this mafucka tamed because we family, baby," he said, and sped up the pace.

I threw my ass back into him, forcing myself to take all of him. I needed to feel that monster in my stomach even deeper. Every time it was my turn, I slammed my ass into him really hard and growled. "Fuck me, J.T., this yo pussy, baby. Fuck this yellow pussy hard. I need that thug passion, that thug love only you can give me!"

He grabbed my hair, making me arch my back. Then, he put my head into the mattress and spread my legs, before fucking me like I was supposed to be fucked. I felt his dick slipping in and out of my walls so fast, I couldn't keep up. All I could do was cry and silently thank the Lord for sending him to me and my cousin.

Afterward, we lay in the bed with me holding his dick in my hand, just playing with it. I couldn't believe it was real, and I had been able to take it all. I was impressed with myself.

He kissed me on the forehead. "Yo, I meant everything I said too. I got you, baby, and I ain't about to let nobody hurt you again. You're special to me. And I protect what's near and dear to my heart. You know, you and Lil' Momma really the only family I got besides my mother, so I need y'all."

I inhaled loudly, and softly blew the air out. I leaned down and kissed his dick head. "Do you think we betrayed her tonight?" I asked, now feeling really guilty. I mean true enough, I had enjoyed everything we did, but now I was really having negative thoughts about the whole ordeal. I wanted to get on the phone and call Lil' Momma, just to tell her what had happened. I didn't think I would be able to keep a secret from her. She meant too much to me. She was my heart.

"Nawl, we ain't betray her. Lil' Momma know what it is, and she know we all family. I'm gon' break shit down to her when the time is right, and I know she ain't gon' sweat it. I mean, that's my baby girl right there and won't nobody ever come before her. But, we're not exclusive. She can do whatever she wanna do, long as she ain't doing it wit some fuck nigga that ain't worthy of her pussy. Then, I gotta step in. But, she got a pretty long leash, we ain't never said we'd be on some one on one shit. Plus, I done told her plenty times about how bad you were to me, so she probably think we fucked last week some time already. Baby don't sweat that petty shit, tho'," he said, and kissed my neck. I was laying on my back and he had my right leg pulled apart from my left, rubbing my naked pussy. It was driving me crazy.

"Well, I hope you're right because the last thing I need to do is lose my cousin. I love her with all of my heart."

He ran his fingers through my hair and kissed my forehead. "And you know what? I love her just as much. I got her, you let me bring this shit to her, okay?"

"Okay."

That night, Lil' Momma woke me up out of my sleep by calling my phone, saying she needed help.

Ghost

Chapter 9
Lil' Momma

"Why do you have to argue with me about everything, Lil' Momma? I mean, everything I say you always have some sort of comeback. Why can't you just keep your mouth closed and do what I say?" my mother asked, and slammed the top to the washing machine.

It had caught me off guard because I had my head in the dryer. So, when I heard the loud noise, I tried to escape it and wound up hitting my head inside of the machine. I was pissed. I took the clothes out and slammed them on top of it. Nothing in the machine was mine, or hers. Once again, we were doing the chores for my punk-ass stepfather. I was over it.

My mother grabbed my arms and I jerked away from her. "Oh, my God. What's gotten into you lately?"

"Yo rapist-ass husband. That's what!" I said, and rolled my eyes.

She grabbed me by my Donna Karan blouse and ripped it. The buttons went flying everywhere. Now, I was really heated. She pressed her forehead to mine. "Listen here, you little bitch. Now, you live in my house, so you gon' respect me and do what the fuck I say, because you are my daughter and that's how it goes."

I tried to knock her hands away, but she was holding onto me too tight. "Let me go, Momma," I said, but my pleas fell on deaf ears.

"No, I'm not letting you go. You're going to listen to me, because you think you're too old for an ass whoopin', but I'll show you real fast that you aren't," she said, looking like an older version of me. We looked exactly alike. My mother was my same height, and maybe weighed five pounds more.

"Momma, I don't think I'm too old to get a whoopin'. I just don't want you snatching me up like you doing. I'm a grown woman and you gotta respect me, just like I'm supposed to respect you."

She tightened her grip, and pulled me closer to her with a menacing look on her face. "When I was little, your grandma let my daddy fuck me and because she did, they had a long and happy marriage. They got the longest marriage in the history of our family. Now, you're acting out because Marvin gets a little taste of you from time to time. Would you prefer that he be out in them streets, cheating on me with every woman he comes across?" she asked, looking at me like I had the problem.

I frowned and knocked her hands away from me. "Get the fuck off of me, you crazy old woman. I can't believe you're trying to sit here and justify your man being a rapist, and a child molester."

She swung and smacked me so hard, I fell to the ground on my knees. Then, she pulled me by the hair, and squatted down.

"Bitch, don't you ever disrespect him like that again, ever in your life! He's been taking care of this family since day-one. And this is the thanks he gets?"

My heart officially broke at hearing her defend him, and completely blow off what I'd just said. It was right in that moment, I understood she would never love me as much as she did him. She didn't care that he had stolen my innocence.

She didn't care that her grown-ass husband had been sleeping with me ever since I was a little girl. She justified it by revealing what my grandmother had done to her. So, as I tried to make it to my feet, I felt the tears wetting my cheeks because I was silently releasing her from my heart.

"Does it matter that he stole my innocence, Mom? Does it matter that he hurt me really bad down there, when I was just a little girl? Does it matter that he used you, just to get to me? That he never saw you standing in front of him, but he always had his eyes pinned on the one that stood behind you? That from day one, he wanted me and not you? Does any of that matter?"

She blinked back tears. "You take that shit back right now, 'cause I know he loves me. He loves me with all of the man he is," she said, crying fully now.

"He never loved you! He only wanted you because you had a little daughter he could molest whenever he wanted to. He knew you were weak. That you were needy, and selfish. Trading your own kid for the happiness of a man. How could you? How could you ever live with yourself?" I screamed.

"Shut up!" she hollered and rushed me with arms swinging.

The first blow caught me in the forehead, and the second busted my lip. I could feel the blood dripping off of my chin. I dropped to the floor and covered my head. I didn't want her to hurt me and mentally, I couldn't see myself putting my hands on my mother as of yet. I still respected her as the one that had given birth to me, even if my love had already faded.

"Get up, you stupid bitch. Get up right now and fight me, since you think you're so grown and you got it all figured out!" She kicked me in the ribs, and knocked the wind out of me.

I rolled over onto my back, and she actually had the nerve to try and stomp me in the stomach. I caught her foot and pushed it backward, making her stumble before bussing her shit. Then I jumped up, and threw up my guards. "I can't believe you just tried to stomp me in the stomach, Momma! How could you?" I screamed, not sure if I wanted to attack just yet. I was going through a crazy battle in my mind. My brain kept on screaming that she was my mother. That I was supposed to honor her and I was never supposed to bring her harm. But, when she punched me in the nose and backhanded me, all bets were off.

I fell down on one knee, and looked up at her with my nose and mouth bleeding. Suddenly, she became the enemy and she was no longer my mother, or a person that I was supposed to have mercy on. I hated her, and I wanted to cause her as much pain as she had allowed her husband to cause me.

I jumped to my feet and bounced on my toes, like a real boxer. "Okay, Momma, you wanna fight, let's get it in. I just want you to know now that after I whoop yo butt, I'm gon' kill you, and then I'm gon' kill yo nigga!"

She rushed me, and I sidestepped her ass and punched her so hard in the jaw, she twisted in the air and landed on top of the washing machine. The sound she made when I first hit her sounded like a yelp, and it broke the virginity of hitting my mother. After that first acknowledgement of pain, I was good to go.

I grabbed her by the hair, and slung her to the ground. She tried to kick at me, but I blocked her assaults and stomped her right in the ribs. "Ooosh!" she groaned, and turned on her side.

"Get yo ass up, Momma! Come on! You been beating me my whole life for nothing. Beating me because your man wanted me, instead of you. It was never my fault. It was yours! You were supposed to protect me!"

She held up her guards, and then started swinging wildly once again. I didn't care, I ran and tackled her ass to the ground so fast and hard that when we landed, her head bounced off of the floor and cracked wide open. Blood began to seep from it, and I didn't care.

I jumped up and ran to the back of the basement, grabbed the fire extinguisher, and ran back over to her as she was just trying to get up. In a bloody zone, I raised it over my head and then brought it down full speed, cracking her right on the side of her forehead. The metal hit her bone with a clunk. She fell on her face and I took the fire extinguisher and brought it down on the back of her head with all of my might. *Clunk!*

"I hate you, Momma! I hate you because you never loved me! You loved your fucking husband more than your own daughter!"

Clunk! That time, it smashed into the back of her head and left it caved in. It looked like her head had been rolled over by a semi-truck. I knelt down and took her by the bloody hair and smashed her face into the ground. "You let him hurt me! You let him steal my innocence! And the whole time, you knew! You knew what was going on!" I slammed her face into the ground repeatedly until I was sitting in a bloody mess.

Five minutes after sitting there and laughing like I was insane or something, I started stuffing her in the dryer. I felt myself cracking. I couldn't stop laughing, and there was nothing funny. My reality was that I had just killed my mother. It seemed like the world started to spin so fast, I couldn't keep up. Yet and still, I couldn't stop laughing, even though I wanted to.

I heard the door slam upstairs. "Anne, I'm home! Where you at, baby?" Marvin hollered.

That stopped the laughing. I felt my eyes get low, and then my upper lip curled. I hated his guts. After switching my clothes into some cleaner ones that didn't have any blood on them, I slipped up the back steps, and into the house, just as Marvin was going into the bathroom to take his after-work shower as he usually did. I could hear the shower water running.

I turned the knob and by no surprise, it opened. I stepped inside of the bathroom and watched him through the shower curtain. He was singing "Honey Love," an old school R. Kelly song, at the top of his lungs.

I had always hated his singing. I hated his voice, and I hated the bitch of a man he was. I flushed the toilet to get his attention.

As soon as it flushed, he pulled the curtain back, and stood before me in all of his fat-ass naked glory. He looked like a black ass, boiled plumber. I couldn't believe I had allowed his chunky ass to get on top of me all of those years. What the fuck was wrong with me? In that moment, I started to actually hate myself. I smacked my hands against my cheek so hard, I tasted blood in my mouth.

He licked his lips. "Say, Lil' Momma. You sho' looking good, baby. What, you thinkin' about taking a shower wit yo Daddy or somethin'?" he asked, grabbing his dick and stroking it. "I sho could use some of that box between them thighs. Lord knows that gap is a blessing."

I smiled, and licked my lips. "I want you to fuck me hard in my mother's bed, Daddy." I lowered my tight ass biker shorts and showed him my naked, brown pussy lips. "Don't you think it's time that you be able to fuck yo daughter all night, instead of having to lay in the bed with that old pussy? Huh, Daddy?" I slid my finger between my sex lips, then opened her up for him to see my pinkness.

He started stroking his dick fast. "Damn, baby, you want me that bad? Since when?" He never took his eyes off of my pussy. He was even slobbering at the mouth like he couldn't control himself and that disgusted me.

I slid two fingers inside myself and pulled them out, sucking my own juices from my fingers. I always loved the way I tasted, and even in that moment, I still did. "I'm feening for you, Daddy. I need you in my mother's bed, right now."

He turned off the shower and started to dry himself off. I walked out of the bathroom with my fingers still up my pussy. Walking bow-legged, making sure he got a good look at my tight ass. I could feel the biker shorts all in my crack too, and I kept them there.

Five minutes later, he came out of the bathroom wrapping a towel around himself. I was waiting on the other side of the doorway. The bathroom door opened outward into the hallway, so in order for him to get out of the bathroom, he had to push the door open.

"Here I come, Princess. Daddy needs that body, and you right too, you should be the one sleeping with me every night. Yo momma done had enough time wit me."

I waited right until he got past the door, raised the crowbar over my head and brought it down with all of my might against the back of his cranium. I mean, I hit his ass hard.

Wham!

He screamed out like a bitch, as blood spurt across my face. Then, he had the nerve to try and run and wound up falling down the stairs, with me on his ass. I watched him tumble down, with blood shooting from the hole in his head. He landed on his face at the bottom, and struggled to get up from a push-up position.

I kicked him right in the ass. "Get yo punk ass up, nigga! You looking like a real bitch right now!" I laughed.

His towel had fallen off, and he was naked as a nudist. "Uh, uh, uh! Why are you doing this, Lil' Momma?" he slurred and tried to get up again, but failed. The hole in his head looked like it was peeing out red Kool-Aid.

I kicked him right in the ass. "Turn yo punk ass over! Right now, nigga!" I kicked him in his ass again. It was already getting ashy. That's another thing I hated about his black ass.

Every time a lick of water touched him, he would get ashy right away. At that moment, his ass looked like he'd sat in some baby powder.

He turned over and I straddled him. "Now, ain't this about a bitch?" I smacked him across the face so hard, he screeched. "I remember you always being on top of me, even when I was bleeding, and now it's yo turn. Funny how life works, ain't it?"

"Princess, I swear, I'm sorry. I won't touch you no more. I won't ever touch you again, I promise," he said, putting his hands up.

I leaned down and bit a chunk out of his face, and spit it on the floor. "Fuck you, you rapist son of a bitch. You ruined me! You made me hate myself! It's because of you that I have never loved myself! Now you want sympathy! Okay, let's have it!"

I flipped him on his back, took the crowbar and forced it up his ass. I used the sharp part too, and made sure I was slamming it hard into him, using all of the muscles I had in my little arm.

"Arrrrrgh! Arrrrgh! Help me! This bitch is fucking crazy!" he hollered and tried to get away from me.

I kept on forcing it into him until blood ran out of his ass, and I could smell shit. He pissed on himself and I kept on going until he just quit struggling. After a while, I figured he was dead, because he had not moved in such a long time. I flipped him over, and started to beat his face again and again with the crowbar until it was a bloody mess. That's when the laughing started all over again, and just like before, I couldn't stop myself from doing it.

Chapter 10
Jennifer

As soon as she opened the door, I grabbed her into my arms. She had tears all over her face, and she was breathing harder than I had ever seen her breathing before. I tried to calm her down. "Lil' Momma, we're here now and it's going to be okay," I said, kissing her on the cheek.

J.T. came over and took her away from me. He wrapped her into his arms and kissed her on the forehead. "Yo, Lil' Momma! Baby, baby, stop all that crying because that ain't gon' solve shit. Like I told you before, you ain't supposed to do nothing you feel gon' make you cry later." He kissed her again and tilted her chin upward to him. "Did you hear what I just said?"

She looked into his eyes and nodded her head. "Yes, baby, I heard you." She sniffed some snot back into her nose, and he kissed her lips.

By the time we got there, she had cleaned up most of the crime scene. The only things left to do was for J.T. to go over it with his sprays and cleaners. Then, we had to get her mother out of the dryer, and her stepfather out of the deep freezer, so we could cut off their limbs and melt their flesh away in the tub.

Three hours later, we were back at J.T.'s crib, eating an extra-large meat lover's pizza, laying on our stomachs on a pallet in front of his big television hanging on the wall in his living room.

He started laughing and bit into one of the slices with so much cheese on it, it was still attached by a thick rope of cheese, even when he pulled it away from the box. He had to wrap it around his fork a few times, before Lil' Momma just up and broke it for him. "Yo, I'm proud of you girls. Now everybody in this living room got at least two bodies under they belt. I don't feel so bad no more," he teased, closed his eyes and took a big bite off of his slice.

I shivered because I still wasn't over the fact that I had killed two people. I was having nightmares every single night about them. Most nights, I couldn't sleep so I had to play with my pussy until I came so much, I exhausted myself and couldn't do nothing else but fall out.

"Damn, J.T., you ain't got no sympathy though. I just kilt my mother for God's sakes. Shouldn't I be feeling some type of way? And if I should, then shouldn't you be consoling me like my man that you are?" Lil' Momma asked, and I could tell that she wasn't joking with him.

He sucked his fingers loudly, and took the two-liter soda pop, and drank right from it. I watched his Adam's apple move up and down. Then he burped and hit himself in the chest with his balled-up fist. "Yo, I got sympathy for you, baby. I'll console you in any way you need me to, come here," he said, pulling her on top of him, and grabbing ahold of her ass.

She had a short, pink Gucci skirt and the more J.T. rubbed on her ass, the further up it went until I could see that she wasn't wearing no panties. His fingers trailed over her sex lips.

"If y'all finna get on that, I'm 'bout to call it a night. I'm tired as hell anyway," I said, standing up and stretching my arms over my head to further drive home my point.

Lil' Momma leaned down and I watched her tongue him like he was her last meal. She opened her legs wider and that made her pussy open up too. I still couldn't believe how slim she was, because looking at her monkey, it didn't fit her body. I didn't know how she walked. It was fat as a boxing glove.

J.T. finished kissing her and looked up. "Why you turning in so early? You know we gotta console her. She been through a lot tonight."

98

"Yeah, and we supposed to be family, Jennifer. Wasn't I there for you when you handled your business?" she asked, sliding her hand into his shorts. I watched her pop his big dick out and start stroking it, like I wasn't even standing there.

"I mean, yeah, Lil' Momma, you were but I just thought that you and J.T. wanted a little privacy. I thought I was being respectful," I said, watching her stroke his monster. My pussy was so wet, I prayed it wouldn't start running down my legs in front of them. I also had on a skirt, but mine was Burberry, and just as short. Every time I moved, it rose on my hips.

"Shid, we ain't got nothing to hide," Lil' Momma said, kissing J.T.'s dick on its head. "Just by you standing where you standing, we able to see all of your yellow pussy, and ain't nobody complaining. Are you, baby?" she asked, before inhaling his pole.

He wrapped her hair into his fist and looked me in the eyes. "Hell nawl, I ain't complaining. I love seeing how fat her pussy is. I can tell y'all related."

That comment made me shiver. I knelt down and my skirt went around my waist, exposing my pussy mound, and I didn't even care. Lil' Momma reached over and slid her hand under my skirt, and I could feel her fingers on my naked sex lips. She squeezed them together, and then slid a finger into me.

I threw my head back. "Ummmmm, shit, Cuz. You betta stop that right now," I moaned and spread my knees further apart. I didn't know what I was getting myself into or why I was behaving like I was. All I knew was I was feeling some type of way about them sexing each other without me. I wanted to be included, and I wanted to feel wanted.

Lil' Momma stopped and ran J.T.'s dick all over her face.

At the same time, she added another finger into my pussy and I lowered myself down onto it, drenching her hand with my juices.

"Damn, Jenn, you're wet. I bet it's because you seeing this big dick in my hand, ain't it?" she said and licked his head.

I crawled over to her and licked her neck. She tasted so good, like forbidden fruit. She moaned and that made me bite her ass, before licking her neck again. "I love you, Lil' Momma. I love you with all of my heart and I'll do anything to console you right now." As soon as the words left my mouth, I knew I was serious. However she needed me, as long as she needed me, I would have done anything she asked.

She moaned. "Come kiss this dick wit me, Cousin." She held J.T.'s dick out to me, pumping it up and down.

I grabbed it and she moved her hand just enough to still share it with me. I leaned forward, and we kissed his dick at the same time, our lips touching each other's. The taboo aspect of it all was driving me crazy.

J.T. reached between my legs, and I felt him playing with my pussy lips. I looked over and saw that he was doing the same thing to Lil' Momma. She closed her eyes and tilted her head back to the ceiling, moaning like he was driving her crazy, so I started to do the same.

She grabbed me by the hair, and we brought our lips together, her sucking all over mine, and me doing the same to her. Our kisses were wet and nasty. Tongues licking each other, before she pulled my halter down, exposing my naked titties. Both nipples were standing up like it was freezing cold in the room.

J.T. slid three fingers into me. "This what I'm talking about. We family! This is how we cement our shit. After we get down, then we jump on our ski-mask shit!"

"Fuck this!" Lil' Momma pushed me back and got on top of me. Leaning down, she sucked on my lips before sliding down my body until her face was between my legs. J.T. helped her spread them, then he pushed my knees to my chest, and Li1 Momma got to slurping all over my pussy.

"Unn, unnn, ohhh shit, Cuz! It feels so good!" I moaned and helped them to hold my legs apart. I needed to come so bad and the way she was eating me, I knew it wouldn't be long before I was.

I grabbed J.T.'s big dick, since it was right by my face and popped it in my mouth, sucking him for all he was worth. He grabbed my hair and did a number on my throat before coming in large globs. I guessed the cousin factor was doing a number on him too.

Lil' Momma sucked on my clit so hard, she sent me into a frenzy. I screamed and started coming, shaking like I had OD'ed or something.

Before it was all said and done, I watched him fuck Lil' Momma from the back so hard, I thought he was hurting her. She slammed back into him with tears in her eyes. I kissed all over his back, and the sides of her ass while he pounded her out.

I wound up fingering myself while I watched them two together. Lil' Momma helped me and every so often, she would suck her fingers.

Before I could get my taste of J.T., there was a beating on the front door. Once again, the first thing I thought about was the police. I figured they had tracked at least one of us down for a murder we had committed.

We got dressed so fast, it was like our parents had pulled up into the driveway and were on their way into the house. After J.T. got his shorts back on, he grabbed two pistols and jogged to the front of the house, stopping in front of the door. "Who is it?"

There was a bunch of muffled sounds and then he swung the door open, and in came a lady looking like she had seen better days. She was about ninety pounds, and had a nappy gray afro. She had on some red snow boots, and keep in mind, it couldn't have been no less than eighty degrees outside. Then, she had on snow pants, and a filthy gray wife beater.

J.T. waved us into the living room, where this lady sat on the couch and crossed her legs. You could actually smell the fish wafting up from her body. "What's going on, Linda?" he asked as me and Lil' Momma came into the living room and stood behind him. "What you beating on my door for, like you the damn police?"

"You got a cigarette?" she asked, smacking her big crusty lips. She gave him a look that said she was praying to the heavens that he did.

J.T. mugged her so serious she looked like she wanted to piss on herself. "I'm not gon' ask you again."

She held up her hand. "Okay, okay. Damn, you always gotta get an attitude, like you hate somebody. I'm the one that done came all the way over here first thing in the morning to let you know that Looney back in town. He got out of prison yesterday and he already got yo momma in that trap house over there in Compton shooting heroin. I personally watched his ass have two dudes hold her down while she shot that shit. Now, she over there fucked up and he ain't trying to let her go nowhere. But, that's not all."

She stopped to check her snow pants. After rummaging around inside of them, she pulled out a sandwich bag of tobacco, and some Tops rolling paper. She poured the tobacco out on the coffee table and rolled her a cigarette. "I don't know why I'm smoking this shit, because it ain't gon' do nothing but give me a headache. Been out on them streets all night, trying to get right and would you believe ain't nobody have a cigarette they could loan me?" She shook her head, and lit the cigarette.

J.T. bent down in her face and grabbed a handful of her afro. "Bitch, why do you keep playing wit me? You think this shit a game?" he asked, snatching her off of the couch, and jacking her up so high in the air, all she could do was kick her dangling feet. "Tell me what the fuck going on wit my mother!"

He dropped her down, and she sat on the floor with her arm around her knees. "Alright, J.T.! Shit! You don't even treat me like yo auntie and I watched yo momma bring you into this world!" She looked up at him with a frown on her face. "He got Jamie in that house too, along with your niece. The last I saw, he was trying to make her start snorting that raw again. I think he wanna turn her back out."

If J.T. hadn't been mad before, now he was fuming. I had never seen his whole face turn red, but that's exactly the shade it was. He paced back and forth with both of the big guns in his hands. "That bitch ass nigga! That bitch ass nigga!" he hollered.

"Who is Looney?" I asked Lil' Momma in her ear. She patted me on the back while she watched J.T. pace back and forth. I could tell she was trying to decide if she should step in and console him or not. "I'll tell you later. But, this isn't good. That nigga, Looney, is a beast just like J.T. They grew up together."

J.T. paused in mid-pace, and mugged Linda. "Is that nigga staying in the same trap?"

She nodded. "Where else he gon' go? That boy been selling dope out of the same house ever since he was a little kid. You should know, all the shit y'all done did in there."

J.T. took a deep breath. "Wait a minute." he said, holding up one finger. He jogged out of the room and disappeared toward the back of the house. He came back about three minutes later, counting a wad of money. "Look, Auntie, I'm about to give you two hundred dollars for now. I just want you to go back to that nigga trap and buy a lil' bit of dope at a time. Don't get greedy, because I'm gon' keep you straight. I just want you to keep an eye on my mother, until I can get her out of there. Tell Jamie I want her to hit my phone ASAP! Tell her it's very important. Can you do that?" he asked, handing her the money.

Her eyes were open so big, it was hard to find her pupils. She looked like a little kid being given a big ole bag of candy. "Yeah, nephew, I can handle that. As soon as I get back in there, I'll relay your message and make sure your momma don't kill herself, fucking with that shit. I got you, baby." She got up and started to walk to the door, stumbling and damn near tripping over her own feet.

As soon as she left, J.T. threw the pistols on the couch, knelt down and tears ran down his cheeks. "Fuck, that bitch ass nigga got my mother and my sister now." He shook his head. "What the fuck am I gon' do?"

Lil' Momma knelt down beside him, rubbing his back. "Baby, I know how you always talked about saving your momma, and getting her out of the hood. But, it's not your fault. You've been doing everything you can for her for as long as I can remember. Sooner or later, she has to be held accountable for her own decisions."

He took a deep breath. "I know, Lil' Momma, but it was my punk-ass father got her hooked on that shit in the first place. She was able to kick the habit one time, but then she turned back to it because I kicked her out of my house, because I thought she stole from me. It turned out that she didn't. My sister did because that nigga, Looney, had her on that heroin shit and I didn't even know it. Then, in regards to her, I'm the one that hooked them two up. If I had never forced the issue, they would have never been together in the first

104

Blast For Me

place, and my sister would have been in college. But, she ain't, because she in this nigga's trap with my six-year-old niece, doing God only knows what. Fuck!"

"Okay, then, let's body that nigga the ski mask way. I mean, because that seems like the only alternative. Fuck it, I ain't about to see my man have a breakdown over this fuck nigga! Let's kill his punk ass." Lil' Momma grimaced.

"Yeah, J.T., she right. It's like you said, we a family, and if somebody hurt one of us, then they gotta pay. I don't know who this dude is, but I'm not afraid to murder him on your behalf, because I know you would do it for me." I knelt down, and kissed him on the cheek.

He took another deep breath, and then stood up. "Look, y'all already know I don't fear no nigga walking this earth. But, y'all also gotta know, I would never allow a mafucka to hurt either one of you in any way." He ran his hand over his waves. "This nigga stupid plugged with them Blood niggaz. I'm talking like, they'll give up they life for him. So, if I wind up going at this nigga's chin over my people, it's gon' be an all-out war, especially if we don't do this shit the right way."

Lil' Momma stood up, and pushed him hard. So hard that he fell backward on the couch, landing on one of the guns. "So, what, nigga, you doubting us now? You lettin' that fuck nigga, Looney, make you second-guess our gangsta?"

He jumped up and got into her face. I didn't know if I should have intervened or what. He gave her a look that said he was ready to kill her and that spooked me.

"Lil' Momma, what I tell you about putting yo hands on me?"

"You ain't tell me shit. Now, answer my question. Do this fuck nigga got you doubting us?" She looked up at him with a slight frown on her face.

She was so small in comparison to him. I knew in one blow, he could damn near knock her head off, and that scared me to death. I loved Lil' Momma with all of my heart, and if it ever came down to it, I would kill anybody over her. I didn't care who that anybody was.

J.T. looked down on her for a long time, and then smiled. "You know damn well I ain't doubting our family. This our cartel right here, baby. If this nigga wanna play crazy like his name, then we about to have a good ass time. Ain't that right, Lil' Momma?" he said and grabbed her into his arms.

"As long as my cousin riding wit us," she said, looking over to me. She held out her arm for me to walk into her embrace. I smiled weakly, walked toward them and wrapped my arm around her shoulder. J.T. repositioned himself to hold both of us.

Chapter 11
J.T.

I should have known it wasn't gon' come down to me having to track Looney down. That nigga was so arrogant and cocky, it was in his nature to parade around with my sister on his arm, just to jack on me.

I grew up with the nigga, and he had been my best friend ever since I was ten years old, and some Latino niggas tried to jump me at school and he jumped in. Back at that time, I wasn't plugged with nothing, but his father was one of the founding members of the Compton Blood Baths, one of the deadliest gangs on California. So, after he helped me fight them niggas, we got cool. Now, due to the fact that I wasn't plugged with shit, them Spanish mafuckas kept getting at my head every day. The school was located on Normandy, and it was in the heart of Latino land. They hated blacks and showed you they hated you, by beating your head in.

Back in them days, my mother wasn't for me missing no school, so I had to show up. Every time I did, the Latinos would jump on me and any other black person that didn't have a crew.

One day, after they had chased me onto the playground and surrounded me, two of them pulled out their little pocket knives. They were ready to cut me up, when Looney and about thirty of his homies stepped in, and we tore that playground up.

One month later, I was plugged into the Blood Baths, and became Looney's right-hand man, after killing his stepfather by blowing his head off with a gauge. He had never done me wrong or nothing. It was just my initiation. Every gang in Cali had their way of jumping you into their gang. Some actually took three or four of its members and they would beat you senseless, until they felt it was enough. Then, they would make you a part of their gang. I never understood this shit. Because if a mafucka jumped me, or hurt me so bad I had to be taken to the hospital, I would hunt they asses until I killed them in cold blood. I would never be able to pledge my loyalty to that gang, so that's what I told Looney, and he honored it. So, instead of that route, I went the route of killing his stepfather, since he didn't like him.

After the murder, me and Looney hit plenty licks together. We started to get our street cred up by being relentless with the pistols. Retaliation was a must at all costs. Both of our tempers were horrible, and we both had this thing for murder.

As hotheaded as we were, we got along and we never got into it, until I hooked him up with my older sister, Jamie, and he started beating her every single day for the smallest things.

At first, I didn't say nothing because he was my mans, and I felt like it was their business. But then, it got to the point that every time I saw my sister, she was fucked up. I was used to her being so pretty, and vibrant. But, after being with him for just six months, she started using and he made sure that he whooped her ass every week.

Long story short, one day I was over at their house and he smacked her in front of me, and I got on his ass. I mean, we tore that house up. I made my sister leave him and I put her in rehab out here in L.A. It took her two years to get clean.

During that time, I was the one raising her daughter, JaMya. Also, during this time, Looney got shot by some niggas over in Long Beach that we grew up with. Since I was still cool with the niggas around the time he got shot up, he swore up and down I had something to do with it, when in actuality, I didn't.

They took him from the hospital bed, straight to jail, where he had warrants for all kinds of shit. He stayed there for eighteen months, in which time I never clapped back at the niggas that popped him. And in Cali, if you don't retaliate against the niggas that got at your peoples, you were pretty much making a statement that the love is lost.

***

Back to the present. We were on our way into the grocery store parking lot, when I looked into my rear-view mirror and saw the nigga Looney's cherry and black, drop-top, '64 Impala, sitting on 188 spokes, with diamond-cut gold bullets. He made it bounce three times, before he pulled on the side of me on three wheels.

He pulled his car up so that his passenger's door was closest to me. I saw Jamie sitting in the passenger's seat with some Ray Bans over her eyes.

"J.T., who is that?" Jennifer asked, touching my shoulder. She was very inquisitive and always had to know what was going on around her. I loved that about her, because it said she was always alert. I needed that in my circle.

"That's that nigga, Looney," I said and rolled down my window. Looney laid back in his seat, and mugged the shit out of me.

He curled his upper lip and then threw up our Blood Bath gang sign. "What up, nigga? Long time, no see."

The sun was beaming like crazy. I had to squint my eyes just to be able to look over to his whip. "When you get out?" I asked, even though I already knew. I was looking at my sister and trying to figure out why she was avoiding any eye contact with me.

"That's the thing. Had you kept shit real, then you would have already known when I was scheduled to touch down. But, you been on some real Crip-type shit lately."

That comment made me wanna go under my seat and grab my TEC-9 and blast his bitch ass. Calling a man a Crip was the biggest form of disrespect. Had my sister not been sitting in his passenger's seat, I would have taken my chances on airing him the fuck out. "Nigga, watch yo mouth."

He started laughing and jumped out of his whip. Since I saw him exiting his shit, I put the .40 Glock on my waist, jumped out of my shit and met him halfway in the parking lot. Around us, people were pushing their shopping carts to their cars and unloading them. Others were going into the big store, and talking amongst themselves. There was a little boy chasing a girl, I guess his sister, into the store. that I guessed was his sister. She was running full speed, laughing and looking over her shoulder. I guessed she wasn't paying attention, because the next thing I heard was *Whoom!* And then, she screamed. I looked and saw she had run straight into the closed glass door. She must have thought it was going to open up once she stepped on the mat, but she had stepped on the wrong side. She stepped on the mat that was for customers leaving, not coming. She laid on the ground crying her eyes out, while her brother tried to explain to his mother that he didn't do anything wrong. She popped him on the back of the head, and they both helped the girl up, before walking into the store.

Looney laughed. "Bitches gotta watch where they going." He looked me up and down. "I'm surprised you still alive. I ain't think you was gon' make it one day without my protection."

"Where my mother at?" I asked, ready to blast this bitch nigga.

He chuckled. "She back at the trap with a table full of dog food. You know I gotta spoil her as much as I can, seeing as she gon' be my mother-in-law real soon." He looked back at his whip and smiled.

"Nigga, I know my sister grown and everything, and she can fuck with any nigga she want to. But, what would make you put her back on that dope shit? Then, I hear you got my mother shooting that poison in her arm now. What's your problem, home boy?" I asked, seconds away from knocking his head off.

He mugged me and curled his upper lip. "Nigga, I ain't got shit to do with what yo momma doing. If she wanna pump that shit into her veins every day all day, I ain't gon' stop her, 'cuz that ain't my responsibility. Far as Jamie go, she do what I do. I like to treat my nose and she do too. I'm her daddy and if she wanna take after me, then that's just what it is, home boy. Why don't you mind yo business, before shit get real ugly for you?" He stepped into my face.

I pushed the shit out of him and upped my pistol, ready to buss his bitch ass. "Nigga, don't you ever step yo soft ass in my face like you forgot how I get down."

I saw him go into his waistband as I raised my gun with my finger on the trigger, then LAPD rolled past on the street behind us, slammed on their brakes, and came flying backward with their car in reverse. The next thing I knew, they were flying into the parking lot. I took off running and so did Looney.

Wurp! Wurp! was the sound that came from their car, indicating that they wanted us to stop running, but I knew better than that. Had them pigs caught us, they was gon' probably see our guns and kill us, and the media would splash our records all over the news, making the cops get away with murder. That's how they got down in L.A.

So, I hit the alley and jumped over the first fence I saw. Looney did the same thing. We wound up in a yard with two big ass Rottweilers. As we were running out of the yard, they were running toward us with their fangs bared. Before I could even buss, Looney shot both of them. *Boom! Boom!* Then, we kept on running, even though I felt pieces of their brains sliding down my leg.

I knew it had to be brain fragments because it felt lumpy and heavy. I ran up on somebody's back porch and kicked their door in so hard, I wound up falling on my face. I was hoping they didn't have any more dogs inside the house.

"Ahhhh!" a Mexican teenaged girl screamed at the top of her lungs. Looney had crashed into the table, sending her breakfast cereal against the refrigerator in their kitchen. She sat still, holding the spoon. Milk was everywhere.

"Aye! Bitch, shut the fuck up before I knock yo head off!" he hollered, pointing his .45 at her.

I bumped him and pushed him into the living room of the house. "Nigga, leave that lil' girl alone, and come on!" I demanded, trying to find their front door. I could hear the sirens of the police car loud as day. I was hoping they didn't have the whole neighborhood surrounded already.

A heavyset Mexican dude with no shirt on, and plenty tattoos ran out of a bedroom, with an old school .38 special in his hand. He aimed it at Looney and fired. *Boom!*

It knocked a chunk out of his shoulder. "Ahhh, you punk ass Mexican!" he hollered and pointed his gun directly at the man before firing. *Boom! Boom! Boom!*

His bullets crashed into the side of the door frame, knocking big chunks of wood out of it. The Mexican man ducked and slammed the bedroom door. I couldn't see if he was hit, because I was already opening the front door of their house.

As soon as I got the door open, a police car rolled down the street, and slammed on its brakes. *Errrrr-uh!* Then, the doors to the squad car opened up and two officers jumped out with assault rifles in their hands.

I slammed the door back, and locked it. Turned around to find Looney laying in the middle of the floor, holding his shoulder. He had so much blood oozing out of him, it worried me some. The last thing I needed was for him to get caught, because he would lead them right back to me in some way, I just felt it.

I knelt down and picked his ass up. "Nigga, get yo ass up, and let's go!" I said, running with him and kicking in one of the bedroom doors so I could find a window to jump out of. It was just my luck the one I chose was a nursery.

A little baby lay in the crib sleeping away, as I pulled up the window and tried to help Looney get out of it. "Come on, nigga! The police out front somewhere, we gotta go now!"

He winced in pain, and pushed me off of him. "Fuck that, Blood. I'm too dizzy. You go and just bail me out if anything happens." He struggled to stand up. "I already know what I gotta do."

The last thing I saw before I jumped out of the window was him picking the baby up out of its crib. I hit the ground, just as two police cars rolled past in front. I ducked low to the ground and ran back toward the backyard. A squad car rolled past the alley, but kept going. I took off running full speed in the direction of the alley, and hopped the gate.

Boy, why did I do that? It was so many police in the alley, it looked like they were having a gang meeting. They had to be about twenty deep. One of them saw me and pointed. "Hey, you, come back here."

I bussed in their direction twice. *Boom! Boom!* And jumped over the neighbor's fence, the next neighbor's fence, and then the neighbor's fence after them, until I got all the way down the block and saw a Mexican man rolling up on a

Ducati. I rushed his ass so fast, and smacked him upside the head with the pistol. He fell off of the bike and I picked it up and jumped on it, popping a wheelie before speeding away from the scene.

Chapter 12
Jennifer

"I'm terrified, Jennifer. I been worrying about him all night. This isn't like him. If there was nothing wrong, he would have been here already. So, there has to be something that went wrong with him," Lil' Momma said, before sitting on the couch.

I walked into the living room and sat on the couch next to her, rubbing her back. "It's gon' be okay, girl. You know he a street nigga. He gon' figure it out. And if anything did go wrong, he know how to navigate them streets. That nigga is a savage!"

She hopped up and ran her hands over her face. "I really wanna believe in what you saying, but I just can't stop my heart from racing. I need my man back in my arms. Being without him is driving me crazy. I mean, what if he's not okay, Jenn? Then what do we do?" she asked, with tears rolling down her cheeks.

As soon as she started crying, then I started. I sensed her vulnerability and that made me lose hope. I knew she knew J.T. way better than me. So, if she was starting to panic, then I felt it was necessary for me to do so as well.

"Let's ask God if he can bring him back to us."

Her head perked up. "Do you think that'll work?"

I shrugged my shoulders. "I mean, it can't hurt." I grabbed her, and we knelt down with our eyes closed. "Okay, so all we have to do is believe in our hearts, and whatever we ask of him, it'll come true. That's what the Bible says, and even though we've been doing a bunch of wrong stuff, I still believe it."

"Okay, well hurry up so it can happen. Ain't no telling where J.T. at right now!" Lil' Momma said, squeezing my hand.

I cleared my throat. "Father, in the name of Jesus, me and my cousin come to you humbly and submissively, and we ask that you receive our prayers. Father, please bring J.T. back home safe to us. We don't know where he is, but we need him to protect us. We know we haven't been doing the right things lately, but we still love you, and we just pray that you forgive us for our sins. Please bring him back to us. Please, Father, we beg of you. In Jesus' holy and precious name, we pray, Amen."

I slowly opened my eyes, and looked down at Lil' Momma. She was still kneeling, with hers closed. I almost started laughing, but thought about J.T. and got sad. "You can get up now, Cuz, damn."

She opened one eye and looked at me. "Is that it? I thought you had to do more than that." Now, she opened both of her eyes and stood up, looking at the ceiling.

"What do you mean, is that it? What all did you think we had to do?"

She shrugged her shoulders. "I just thought that since we've been doing so much, it would take longer for prayers to get to him. Or we would have to do a lot of extra stuff."

"Well, thankfully, it isn't that difficult. Now all we do is let him answer our prayers," I said, sitting down on the couch, feeling sick over J.T. again. We had already seen on the news that Looney had been snatched up after a brief standoff with the police. They apprehended him after he passed out from blood loss. The news anchor said the police were looking for his accomplice. They said he was being charged with home invasion, recklessly endangering safety, attempted murder on

116

a police officer, and cruelty to animals, resulting in the death of them. All serious felonies in the state of California.

So, I was spooked. I didn't know how me and Lil' Momma was going to make it in such a cold, cold world.

I damn near had a heart attack when the front door to J.T.'s house opened and slammed, and he walked into the living room.

He had a ski mask over his face. "Yo, get some clothes and let's get the fuck out of here, them people on my ass!" he hollered and ran into his bedroom.

Me and Lil' Momma got to scrambling and snatching up clothes, stuffing them into suitcases. My heart was beating so fast, I thought it was about to go out on me. It felt like somebody was kicking me in the chest.

"Baby, where are we going?" Lil' Momma asked, trying to pick up her big ass suitcase, but couldn't.

"We finna shoot over to Vegas for a few weeks until shit die down over here. If we stay in Cali, I'mma be in jail by the morning. And all that shit they trying to charge me with gon' fuck me over," he said, picking up Lil' Momma's suitcase.

We pulled up in Vegas hours later and were met by the bright lights. I stood looking out of my window, amazed. I had never been there before, or anywhere outside of California, for that matter. I could see the bright lights of the Sunset Strip in the distance and I wanted to go there immediately.

"Oooh, baby, can we go do some gambling, and sightseeing?" Lil' Momma asked, with her head sticking out of the window. She acted like she was just as excited as I was.

"Yo, once we get settled in, we can do all of that. But for right now, we gotta get ourselves together. We only got ten G's to our names."

"Ten stacks! Why is that?" Lil' Momma asked, with a look that said she was ready to panic.

"Because my safe's in my mother's crib in the floor. When I went over there, the police were all over her spot. It was no way I was gon' be able to get to that safe without getting popped off. So, we at ten G's."

She plopped back into her seat and crossed her arms. "I ain't never known you to be so careless. Why the fuck you only got one stash spot? We can't do shit wit ten bands. That shit will be gon' in a day or two, especially since we ain't got no clothes like that."

I wanted to say something to defuse the bomb that was sure to go off, but I also didn't want to get into their argument. The last thing I needed was for them to kick me to the curb. So, I just hung back and kept my comments to myself, although I did think my cousin was being a brat.

He frowned and gave her a sad look. "Thanks for making me feel worse than I already do. You know I don't like feeling like a failure."

"Well, this one time you should, because you dropped the ball. How you gon' make sure everybody straight on ten thousand, weak-ass dollars." She gave him a face that said she was disgusted.

He nodded. "You right, boo. But, I got some shit lined up, and we just gon' have to get our feet dirty right away out here. Once we got at least thirty stacks, then we can go hit up a casino or something."

"Now, you talking like my man," Lil' Momma said, smiling.

I'm thinking the whole of Las Vegas was all glitz and glamour. That they didn't have no ghetto parts to it, because you never heard about it being advertised. But boy, was I wrong.

We pulled up in a neighborhood so grungy, it made L.A. look like the suburbs. The neighborhood was full of apartment buildings that had been boarded up, and they all looked run down.

They had niggas in the middle of the street with blue rags on their heads and faces, and what blew my mind was that they actually had their guns in hand, like it was the Wild West or something.

All along the street was broke down cars, that looked like they had been stripped and left there after being stolen. The grass had big patches in the middle of each building's lawn, and the sidewalk was torn up. It looked like a bunch of people had been going around, smashing it with a sledgehammer every day.

When J.T. hit his turn signal to turn down this block with all of the dudes in the middle of the street, I damn near shit on myself. I thought that he was making a mistake.

Lil' Momma reached under her seat and put a gun on her lap. "If one of these niggas even move the wrong way, I'm blowing they head off," she said through clenched teeth.

She had more heart than me at that time, because I was thinking if one of them niggas moved the wrong way, I was gon' piss on myself and J.T.'s seat, at the same time. So, I was already trying to figure out how my apology was going to go.

I was shaking and everything. I felt like we were driving over a bridge that was about to break. As we pulled onto the block, some high-yellow nigga about my complexion, upped an assault rifle at the car and directed us to pull to the side of the street. When he did this, about six other dudes surrounded our car.

"J.T., I'm finna buss one of these niggas fa real," Lil' Momma said. "You betta tell me something." She cocked the pistol and put it between her legs.

J.T. smiled. "Yo lil' ass turning into me more and more every single day." He leaned over and kissed her. "We good, these my people right here." He threw the car in park, and got ready to open his driver's door.

Lil' Momma shook her head. "Wit all that blue on? Nawl, that don't seem right to me. Ever since I known you, you been bloody as a bandage. These niggas true blue out here, so something ain't right."

He squeezed her thigh and rolled down his window. The light-skinned nigga stuck his head in. "Yo, what up, Cuz? What you doing in town?"

"I need asylum for a week or so. Some crazy shit done happened back home, so I need to lay up wit my peoples." He pointed with his head to me and Lil' Momma.

The yellow nigga looked us over closely, and turned his eyes back on J.T. "Cuz, we at war wit the Bloodz heavy right now. It ain't safe over here. I'd be lying if I told you that it was."

J.T. shook his head. "I don't give a fuck, we can handle it. Huh, this ten G's right here. All I need is a week in yo jungle and we'll be on our way. Give me a room in one of those back buildings."

The yellow nigga nodded, and did some sort of signal. As soon as the apartment door opened, a rat ran at me that was so big, I thought it was a possum. It was screeching and running in a zig zag. I damn near fainted. I hated rats and anything too small for me to kill right away.

Lil' Momma jumped on J.T. and he caught her. "What the fuck was that, J.T.?" she hollered.

He put her back down. "Chill out, baby. That wasn't nothing but a lil' rat. It ain't shit. Now, y'all step in and quit being so fucking dramatic." He moved to the side so that me and Lil' Momma could walk into the empty apartment.

It had old newspapers and beer bottles all over the floor. I figured it had been a hangout for some of the teens in the hood we were in. It smelled like plenty weed smoke, which didn't bother me. I was just wondering where we were going to sleep, because if it was the floor and the place had rats as big as the one that had run out of it, then I was going to have a problem getting to sleep. "Uh, J.T., are we sleeping on the floor?" I asked, watching what looked like a hundred roaches crawl across it.

"Hell, nawl! I know I ain't. I don't give a fuck who looking for us. I ain't sleeping on this infested ass floor. And J.T., you know better than this," she whined.

He lowered his head. "Damn, this ain't gon' be easy, is it?"

"Nawl, and you just gave dude our last ten bands. You better go and get it back and tell him we cool," Lil' Momma said, serious as hell.

J.T. nodded. "Okay, look, let's just get some rest. Even if we gotta stand up to do so. Let me collect my thoughts and then we can get up out of here first thing in the morning. Bet?"

All I could do was exhale and look at all of the roaches. We couldn't even make it to the morning, before there was a beating on the door. It happened about two hours after we'd gotten there. Lil' Momma got up and answered the door because J.T. was in the bathroom, taking a shit.

"Who is it?" she asked.

"It's Petey, the same nigga that approved for y'all to stay here."

I don't know why she did it, but the next thing I saw, she was opening the door. As soon as she did, that same yellow nigga came in with two guns raised. "Lay it the fuck down, Cuz!"

I wanted to cry right away. I got down on my stomach, laying right on a pile of roaches. I could feel them crawling all into my shirt, and down my bra. It felt like I was being tickled by a bunch of feathers. I was seconds away from freaking out.

"Where the fuck J.T. at?" he asked, looking down at me.

Chapter 13
J.T.

As soon as I hear a mafucka say, "Lay it down," I pulled up my boxers. I hadn't even gotten the chance to shit yet. I grabbed both of my .40 Glocks, and put my ear to the bathroom door, trying my best to hear what was going on.

"Where the fuck J.T. at?" I heard a nigga ask. That let me know it was a hit, and it had to be some inside shit going on. There were only a few people that knew I was in Vegas, and none I trusted.

I opened the window to the bathroom, and wiggled my way out of it. I didn't even have time to put no shoes on. But I didn't care, because time was of the essence. As soon as I dropped down into the alley, I took off running full speed until I got around to the front of the building. I didn't even take time to dwell on the fact that I was stepping on rocks and shit. The only thing on my mind was getting to my girls before something bad happened to them. I would've never be able to live with myself, because they were my responsibility and it was my job to protect them at all times.

When I got back around to the front of the building, I ran inside the door and back up a flight of stairs. Our apartment was the first one as soon as you got to the top of the stairs. I saw the door wide open and the sound of muffled voices coming from inside of it. I shot up the stairs and ran right through the door, with my mind set on bussing the first nigga I saw. I was gon' blow his muthafuckin head right off of his shoulders and keep it moving.

But, when I got inside of the spot, the first person I saw was my cousin. He was standing facing the door, holding two big ass .44 Bulldogs, waiting for me to come through it. He had a big ass smile on his face, and even though I knew it was all a game now, I wanted to knock his head off.

Lil' Momma was on the floor, lying on her stomach with her arms stretched over her head. Jennifer was the same way. I knew my cousin might have thought it was all fun and games, but I was sure my girls didn't. We had been through too much shit for him to be playing around like he was.

"Rip, why you playin' 'n shit, nigga?" I asked, with my guns pointed at him. As soon as Lil' Momma heard my voice, she turned around onto her back and got up and ran to me.

"You know this bitch ass nigga, J.T.?" she asked, looking at him like she wanted to kill him in cold blood. She frowned up her face, then went and helped Jennifer to her feet.

"Yo, I was jus' playin' around to try and see if you was still on yo toes after all these years. Come on, now. You got these lil' bitches out here, guarding the door wit no pistols. Any mafucka could have come in and knocked they shit loose, and then caught you slipping in the bathroom." He put his guns on his waist.

I waved that nigga off and went over and hugged Lil' Momma. "Baby, you good?" I asked, before kissing her on the forehead.

She closed her eyes and nodded. "I don't understand why you got niggas that play games like this. Then, this nigga callin' us bitches and shit. What's he on?" she asked, looking offended.

"Yeah, J.T., this ain't cool. I damn near had a heart attack, and all for what?" Jennifer said, wrapping her arm around the small of my back. I could still feel her shaking, and that pissed me off.

I released them and walked over to my cousin and bussed him in his jaw, hitting him so hard he fell down to one knee.

"Fuck wrong wit you, nigga? We don't play them kind of games and you already know that."

He put his hand to his jaw after spitting blood onto the floor. "Nigga, I said I was sorry. Damn!" He slowly got to his feet, and mugged the shit out of me.

Lil' Momma turned her nose up at him. "Nigga, that's what you get for playin' them childish ass games. What if one of us was packin' and we had blasted yo fool ass? Then what, huh?"

He shrugged his shoulders. "I guess I'd be a dead ass nigga, then. It is what it is."

"Alright, so ain't too much changed since you been gon'. We still beefin' with Kelly and nem, but now they got a few plugs comin' out of Arizona that keep them laced with the best heroin, and some high-powered assault rifles. They still screamin' Crip too, even though they ain't at none of the picnics or fundraisers for the mob. I know you used to fuck wit his sister, Veronica and it may sound crazy, but that's his right hand now. She actually bussing more moves than he is, 'cuz the Greek nigga she fuckin' with now must have come out here to Vegas while she was working the strip and took a likin' to her. He took her back to Arizona for about six months after they left here, and the next time I saw her, she was rollin' a Rolls Royce," Rip said handing me a stuffed blunt of Tropical Loud.

He continued. "She snatched up Kelly, took him down there and when they got back, the next thing I knew that fool was rolling a Range Rover on the weekdays, and a Bentley on the weekends. All his niggas eatin' now. And every so often, they let them shots ring in the air just to let mafuckas know what they bussin' over there. That nigga got two heroin houses, and a gambling spot where they don't deal with shit, but cash. I wanna hit at least one of them before you head back west."

I took the blunt from him and handed it down to Jennifer. She smiled and laid her head on Lil' Momma's shoulder. Quiet as it's kept, I was starting to feel her lil' fine ass more and more lately. I mean, not to the point I was ready to kick Lil' Momma to the curb, or nothing like that. I was just starting to pay more attention to the sexy movements and ways she had about herself. She was very seductive, and I didn't even think she noticed it about herself.

"Fuck robbin' one spot, we gon' hit all three of they asses if I got anything to say about it."

Rip shook his head as if he needed to stop me in my tracks. "Cuz, it ain't that type of party. That nigga ain't sweet like you remember him. Now, he got goons everywhere and they 'bout that action. Us being able to hit one of the spots gon' be a stretch. That's why we gon' have to do it during his sister's birthday bash, or else we ain't gon' be able to make shit shake. You gotta listen to me on this. I know what I'm talkin' about. You been gone, I ain't," he said, reaching his hand into the McDonald's bag and pulling out a Big Mac.

He opened his mouth wide and took a big bite out of it, like he was starving or something, chewing with his eyes closed.

Lil' Momma stood up and rubbed my back. "Baby, I know y'all talkin' business right now, but I just want you to remember you got two bad bitches with you. If you thinkin' we can hit all three of them spots, then we rollin' with you. After that fuck shit he did earlier, I wanna wet some shit up anyway. Maybe if I can body somethin' out here, it'll cleanse my conscience of the shit that's already on it, drivin' me crazy." She laid her head on my chest.

Rip looked her up and down and licked his lips. "Damn, shorty bad as a muthafucka, Cuz. She is too," he said, pointing at Jenn with his head. "Where you find them at?"

I grunted and almost said something to him that was disrespectful. "These my people right here and they been wit me since day one. They was just ducked off, which is why ain't nobody ever knew about them. This ain't that, though."

"Aw, nawl, I wasn't sayin' it like that. I was just tryin' to figure out what was good wit 'em, 'cuz I ain't never seen you rock wit nobody on that level, other than that nigga, Looney. And even then, you and homie wasn't all that tight. I mean, I peeped that from a distance."

It was just like Rip to always think he got shit all figured out when he didn't. You see, Rip was my Auntie Linda's son. He'd always come to L.A. for the summer when we were kids, or I'd go over and spend the summer with him and my Auntie out in Vegas.

Me and him was never really tight like that. We were both stick-up kids. So, when he came to L.A., I'd put him up on licks, and when I came out to Vegas, he'd do the same for me.

That's where I met Veronica. She was sorta like my summertime honey and we only fucked around heavy on that level, around that time. But, when the summer ended, so did our relationship until the following summer. I ain't fuck wit her brother, Kelly, because that nigga was Crip, and back in L.A., I was knocking they heads off on a daily basis.

"Well, times have changed. We the ones that's holdin' him down now. And I'll buss my gun just like any nigga would, all a mafucka gotta do is try me, or try them," Lil' Momma said, glaring at Rip with hatred in her eyes.

"Whoa, whoa, whoa," he said, holding his hands in front of him. "I ain't doubtin' you, baby girl. I can tell that you 'bout that life. Calm down, we all family here."

She rolled her eyes. "It's only two people in my family, homie, and you ain't neither one of them."

"Damn, it's like that?"

"It's just like that until you prove yourself. Right now, yo image tainted in my eyes 'cuz of that childish shit you did. I ain't never met a boss nigga that got down like that. So, I'm findin' it hard to take you serious."

"Me too. I'm tryna figure out why J.T. even fuckin' wit you on that level," Jennifer said, handing the blunt to Lil' Momma.

I laughed. "Y'all should already know that if I'm rockin' wit any nigga, family or not, they gotta be up on they shit, 'cuz I don't fuck wit niggas. My lil' cousin was just on some dumb shit and we ain't gon' hold that against him. Everybody deserve a second chance until they don't, ya feel me?"

***

"How long we gotta follow this fuck nigga, Rip? We been behind this nigga for two hours. If you sayin' he be doin' the same shit every day, and so far he ain't stepped outside of that, then we good to go."

Rip curled his upper lip. "Trust me, Cuz, you gotta take this nigga more serious now. I'm just makin' sure he not steppin' outside of his usual game plan. Any mistakes we make could be very costly. I told you, he ain't really workin' for himself no more. He plugged in down south. I don't know who his connects is. I just know they gotta be Greek."

I was hearing him talk, but at the same time, I knew I was on the clock. I couldn't stay in Vegas that long. It would be only a matter of time, before the police was out here looking for me. They always traced where your people stayed first. And, I had been released on probation to my aunt's crib out here in Vegas one time, so I was sure that if they did their homework, it wouldn't be long before they were trying to track me down there.

"Aiight, it's good. Now, that nigga finna get on a plane, and be gone for two days. By the time he gets back, we should have hit at least two of his spots, even though I'm tellin' you, we should leave it at one."

We watched Kelly get out of a purple Bentley, and slam the door. He popped the trunk and pulled out a Louis Vuitton suitcase, strapping it around his shoulder. A thick ass Puerto Rican female got out of the passenger's seat, with a tight yellow Prada dress on. She shuffled into his arms and he wrapped them around her and they tongue-kissed each other for what seemed like three minutes. I watched him grab her big ass booty and grope all over it, before they parted, and he walked into the airport.

"That's his baby mother right there. He bumped that bitch on the island. Now she finna roll back to his crib on Cherry Avenue. He got a safe in there that got about ninety G's in it. I know that ain't much money, but it's a start. I got some unfinished business with this bitch anyway, so we can kill two birds wit one stone."

I didn't give a fuck what he had going with her. All I heard was that it was supposed to be ninety G's in the house and I wanted my share. That would be forty-five bands, but cut between me and my girls, that was only fifteen apiece, so that was chump change.

For all of the money this nigga Kelly had, his security detail for his woman was weak as hell. As soon as she pulled up in the garage, we pulled right in behind her and boxed her in.

Rip got out of the car with his white ski mask on and so did I. As soon as she opened the driver's door, he snatched her up, and I kicked in the door that led from the garage into the house. I was met by a big ass pitbull that caught me off guard.

It got to growling and running right at me. I aimed straight at it and bussed. *Boom*! Knocking its heart out the back of it. Rip had the bitch with his arm around her neck. He dragged her into the house and slung her to the floor. She landed right on top of the dead dog, and started to freak out.

"Arrrgh, oh my God," she said, shaking on the floor. She jumped up, wiping her ass off. She kept her eyes fixated on the dog and began freaking out. "You killed Papi! You killed Papi. Why did you kill my dog, you sonofabitch?" she screamed and lashed out at Rip, swinging her arms wildly.

He grabbed her by the throat and slung her into the pantry. I watched him smack her so hard, she fell against a bag of flour. It fell to the floor and burst, sending white smoke into the air. He grabbed her up by her hair and stuck his .45 into her face. "Bitch, I ain't got time fo' this shit. Take me right upstairs to the safe and get me the money. I already know it's up there and how much. If you play wit me, I'm knocking yo brains out. Now, let's go!" He threw her in front of him by her hair.

"Okay, but stop touchin' me, you sick bastard. Do you even know who you're rippin' off? Don't you know that all of this money belongs to the cartel? When they find out who you are, you're dead men, both of you," she said through clenched teeth.

"Shut up!" he said, kicking her in the ass.

I surveyed the area very carefully. The last thing I needed was for something or somebody to jump out at me. The crib was laced like a muthafucka. Everything was all-white, and Kelly had all kinds of famous paintings hanging on his walls.

The floors were marble, just like the counters. There were big flat screens everywhere, and it just looked like a place I would have chilled at, whenever I wanted to escape my own world of pain.

She led us up the stairs, and into a narrow hallway that led to a linen closet. Once there, Rip threw her to the floor and tore it apart. Throwing towels and sheets out, he squatted down and pulled a big safe out of it.

"Here this mafucka go right here, Cuz," he said, grunting as he pulled it further into the hallway.

The Puerto Rican bitch had the nerve to get up and start running back the way we came, but I was on her ass. Before she could even make it to the staircase, I leaped and tackled her ass to the carpet, us falling with a loud thud.

She started punching at my head and face, and I had wished Lil' Momma was there, because I would've had her fuck this bitch up royally. "Get off of me, you bastard. Let me go. Let me go, right now! I'm not openin' that fucking safe, because you're going to kill me anyway!" she screamed.

"Man, beat that bitch, Cuz. Stomp that bitch in her shit. I bet she'll act right then," Rip said, standing up.

As much as I knew what he was saying was one hunnit, I never could beat no female. That shit just wasn't in me like that. Whenever I even thought about hitting one, I started to feel like a sucker ass nigga, so I never could bring myself to do it. That's where Lil' Momma came in at, because she ain't have no problem getting knee deep in a bitch's ass, and I ain't have no problem letting her.

"Please, don't hurt me is all I'm sayin'. I'll tell you everything. I'll get you the fuckin' money, just don't kill me please, because I don't have anything to do with this," she whined, looking at me and pleading her heart out.

Rip came over and grabbed her by the hair and dragged her all the way down the hallway with no mercy. "Bitch, I ain't got time for this shit. Get yo punk ass over here and open this

mafuckin' safe, before I beat you until you black and blue!"
He slung her in front of the safe like a rag doll.

"Okay, I'll open it, just please don't kill me," she begged,
crawling to the safe and opening the control panel so she could
get to the keypad to enter the combination. She looked up to
Rip one last time with tears in her eyes, before entering the
combination. "Please, just promise me that you won't kill me
once you get the money that's inside of it. I shouldn't have to
die when none of this has anything to do with me."

Rip knelt down right next to her, and put his mouth to her
ear. "Bitch, I'm gon' tell yo punk ass one more time to open
that muthafuckin safe. If I have to tell you again, I'm splashin'
you. Now, that I can promise you!" he growled through
clenched teeth.

She nodded and began to punch in the code. No more than
ten seconds later, the safe was open and I was throwing all of
the cash inside into a pillowcase I had taken from one of the
bedrooms. There were also a few pistols inside, as well as a
few pieces of jewelry that looked like it cost homeboy a pretty
penny. Once I got everything, I was ready to go.

"Yo, let's go, bro. We out this mafucka," I said, heading
to the stairs. I looked back over my shoulder and saw that he
had his pistol shoved all the way down the chick's throat.

"Aiight, Cuz, go 'head. I'mma meet you downstairs." I
saw him take a minor step back, and then *Boom*! He splattered
her brains against the wall in the hallway. It looked like a
tomato had exploded. He looked down at her, and then ran
toward the stairs.

I took one last look at our victim before we ran out of the
house and jumped in the whip, where I stepped on the gas until
I got to the freeway, on my way back to Jennifer and Lil'
Momma.

Chapter 14
Lil' Momma

"Damn, girl, wake yo ass up!" J.T said, smacking me on the ass. I jumped up dizzy as hell, probably because I'd gotten up too fast. I tried to gather myself, but had to immediately sit back because nausea had taken over me.

Over the last three days, I had gotten about three hours of sleep total. There were so many things racing through my head that I couldn't slow my mind down enough to fall asleep. When I finally did feel at ease enough to fall out, here J.T. was, smacking me so hard on my ass it made me want to whoop his.

He knelt down beside me. "Baby, what's wrong? Are you sick or somethin'?" he placed the back of his hands on my forehead, I assumed to check my temperature.

I shook my head. "No, I'm not sick. I just feel really dizzy right now. I must've stood up too fast." I lowered my head as I felt him rubbing my back.

"Yeah, well, I hope you ain't getting' sick because I need your strength right now. We got a lot of business to handle out here in these streets and I don't trust no mafucka to have my back like you do. Here." He dropped a bunch of hundred-dollar bills in my lap as he stood up, stretching his arms over his head.

If I wasn't feeling good before, I definitely was after seeing all them big-faced hundreds. I got to counting them right away, licking my thumbs and everything. I couldn't stop the huge smile from spreading across my face either.

"You ain't gotta count it again, 'cuz I already have a few times. That's sixty G's right there. It was supposed to only be forty-five, but I let my cousin keep some jewelry and shit that I didn't care about. You already know we supposed to take cash over everything else." He knelt down on the pallet I had made in the middle of the living room floor, yawning. "I'm tired as a muthafucka. Do me a favor and wake me up in three hours. I'on need to sleep no longer than that, Aiight?" With that, he closed his eyes.

"Yeah, J.T., I got you. Get some rest, 'cuz I need you to be on yo game. You hear me?" His only response was his loud ass snoring. That's how I knew he was tired. Of all the times I'd been around him, he only snored when he went days without sleep.

Jennifer stepped into the living room, and froze in her tracks as she looked to see all the money in my lap. "Damn, girl, what he do, go out there and rob a bank or somethin'?" She ran her tongue across her juicy lips, got down on all fours, and crawled across the floor to me. "How much is here?"

"J.T. says it's only sixty G's, but I'mma count it again to make sure. He seemed like he was physically exhausted, so I wanna make sure he didn't make any mistakes." I put all of the money into a pile and started to count it out, making five-thousand-dollar piles.

Jennifer grabbed a pile and repeated the same steps, with the end total being sixty-one thousand dollars. I nodded, silently impressed with how J.T. went out in them streets and made shit happen. In my opinion, that was what separated the men from the boys, especially if you were a boss ass nigga. Only scrub bitch niggas made excuses, and were always broke. How a man could allow himself to walk around like a bum, and not use every means he had to make it happen, was beyond me. But those kind of men, I despised, and they'd never be allowed to lay a finger on me.

"I'm fuckin' starvin'. We gotta go out and get somethin' to eat soon," Jennifer said, rubbing her stomach. "I could eat a whole horse by myself right now. Shit, the horse and the damn jockey that rides it," she joked.

I couldn't help but bust out laughing, being that I was just as hungry. Even though I was a slim female, I kept a healthy appetite when my emotions were in check. Hell, I would've fought Jennifer to the death, just to kill the horse first, so that I could take a huge bite out of its ass. "I saw a Subway 'bout a block over, you wanna walk over there and order some food?" I asked, stuffing a hundred dollars in my bra.

"Babe, at this point, I'll literally eat from anywhere. Even those roaches starting to look good." She licked her lips as we watched about six roaches crawl across the floor so fast, it looked like they were racing each other. As soon as Jennifer peeped one crawling close to J.T., she stomped on it, causing the others to scatter in the opposite direction.

***

The sun hit me right in the face as soon as I stepped out of the apartment. It was extremely humid and felt like damn near a hundred and ten degrees, and sweat immediately formed on my forehead, pooling on the side of my face. The humidity made it almost impossible to breathe. It was like being in the trunk of a hot car without an escape.

"Fuck, it's hot out here." Jennifer had turned a bright shade of pink as she popped her shirt collar, her tongue hanging out her mouth. Beads of sweat began to form on her forehead as well, and a look of irritation set on her face as she tried her best to keep her gelled baby hairs laid. "Why the fuck is it so hot?" she whined, fanning her face.

"I don't know, but let's hurry up and go get some food so we can get our asses back inside. It didn't seem like it was as hot inside, did it?"

She shook her head and wiped sweat off her forehead. We waited until a car drove past then crossed the street, where we noticed quite a few little girls jumping Double Dutch on the sidewalk. They had a huge pitcher of ice-cold lemonade sitting on the porch behind them and it looked good as hell. As petty as it sounded, I wanted to take my .380 and rob they asses.

"Damn, that shit look good, don't it, Lil' Momma?" Jennifer pointed to the tall pitcher. Clearly, we were thinking the same thing. She looked like she wanted to rob their asses, too.

"Hell yeah, I was just thinkin' that shit. We should jack they lil' asses for it." I was serious as a heart attack. It irritated my soul as I watched a lil' chubby girl pour her a cup, pausing between sips. Man, that made me envious.

"Lil' bitch!" Jennifer mugged the shit out of the girl. We laughed all the way to Subway, realizing how petty we would have been to mess with them lil' girls.

"Damn, it feel good in here." Jennifer welcomed the cool air into her shirt as we felt it smack us in the face, when we walked through the door. I had to agree. I felt like a slave who had just been granted their freedom.

"Uh-uh, if you guys aren't buyin' anything, I'd advise y'all to go back out in that heat. I mean, I don't wanna come off rude, but this is a place of business, not a shelter," spoke a heavyset and ugly black woman. She was so ugly, children could use her face as a Halloween mask, and to make matters worse, she had the nerve to have on bright red lipstick.

I strolled over to the counter, looking at her like she'd lost her fucking mind. It was so hard to support black-owned establishments. Why be in customer service if you had a fucked-up attitude? This broad knew how hot it was, yet she had the audacity to come at us sideways. "Damn, can we have a seat for a few seconds, without you being all mean and shit?" I questioned, rolling my eyes.

"I don't know you," she replied, swatting a fly out of her face, "but rules are rules. If somebody else see y'all just sittin' in here 'cuz of the heat outside, then folks gonna bring their ratchet ass in here and do the same fuckin' thing. I ain't got time to be babysittin' this whole ass hood." She rolled her eyes back, looking like an irritated gorilla. "Now, can I take ya order? Or are y'all leavin' the store?"

"Aye, don't be talkin' to my cousin like that. I don't know who you think you are, but you betta have more respect than you showin'. We 'bouta order our food. We just needed to take a seat, 'cuz of the effects the heat had on us."

The gorilla mugged the shit out of Jennifer, then laughed, causing her stomach and everything in her too-small uniform shirt, to vibrate. Her frame looking like that of a minivan. "I'm supposed to be scared of yo pretty ass? Bitch, if you don't get outta ma face, I'mma jump over this counter and whoop you and her." I saw her point in my direction. "Between her skinny ass, and yo yellow ass, I'll take my chances." She laughed so loud with her mouth wide open, I wanted to pull out the gun in my waistband and empty it right down her throat.

"Who you callin' a bitch?" Jennifer stepped closer to the counter, her face red-hot, jaw clenched and both fists balled up.

The gorilla pursed her lips, and sucked her teeth loudly. "Like I said, am I supposed to be afraid or somethin'?" She pretended to yawn, placing her hand to her mouth to mock us.

"Bitch, you ain't gotta be scared of a muthafuckin' thing, but you gon' respect the both of us or it's about to be some problems up in here!" On behalf of Jennifer and myself, I was ready to kill this ho for her blatant disrespect. This hatin' ass bitch was trying to flex on us because of our small frames and good looks, but she just didn't know that Jenn and I were both packing. We'd happily knock the head off her shoulders, jump behind that counter and make our own sandwiches. This shit wasn't a game.

"Say, lil' girl, I ain't gotta respect neither one of you bitches, so make yo next move yo best move, or hurry the fuck up and order yo food, and make yo way outta the store. Y'all stankin' up the freshness in here."

A light-skinned sistah, smaller than her, came from out the back with her red hair whipped. She had freckles all over her face and a small scar on her forehead. "Shirley, what's goin' on up in here?" She looked from her to us.

"What's goin' on is, this bitch 'bout to get her head blown off if she don't get her shit together. She comin' at me and my cousin real reckless, and if she wasn't in this store, she would have already been taken care of."

The lil' freckle-faced, light-skinned chick looked back at Shirley. "What she talkin' about, because it definitely ain't that type of party in here. Ain't nobody gon' put they hands on my woman." She began taking off her earrings, setting them on the counter.

Shirley waved us off. "These ratchet ass hoes ain't on shit. They just talkin' 'cuz they stupid. They don't know who they fuckin' with," she said, slamming her hand onto the counter, startling me a little bit.

"I'll tell ya what. Fuck both you bitches. If y'all wanna do somethin', all y'all gotta do is lock the door, turn the camera off, and we can tear this mafucka up. Right now!" Jennifer removed her earrings. "Bitches always think 'cuz I'm pretty, that it's a game. I'mma show you hoes what's really good."

"You bitches bad! Lock them doors, and turn them cameras around, so we can see what y'all about. You hoes think it's sweet 'cuz y'all fat. So, what's up?" I questioned, slamming my hand on the counter, catching Shirley off guard.

The light-skinned broad curled up her lip. "You know what, it's been a minute since I done got into a bitch's ass, and I definitely deserve this. Shirley, turn them cameras around. Don't no mafucka come up in ma store and stand on me! Fuck they think this is?" She walked from behind the counter, past me and Jennifer.

My eyes grew buck from excitement as I watched the broad walk from behind the counter by her lonesome, not knowing that Jenn and I were plotting. These bitches really thought it was sweet.

Jenn and I made eye contact and the look she gave me, confirmed it was time to have some fun. My adrenaline kicked in, and that made it hard for me to breathe. I watched the gorilla stand on her tiptoes and turn the camera towards the wall, unplugging it as well.

The light-skinned girl made her way back over toward the cash register, about to pass Jennifer and me when, *Wham!* Jennifer's fist connected with the light-skinned chick's chin, knocking her clean the fuck out, sending the chick crashing to the floor on her back, and shocking the hell outta me.

"You punk bitch! I love it when hoes underestimate me." Jennifer straddled the chick, punching her repeatedly in the face, her hair coming out of its ponytail, falling all over her face.

That shit got me geeked. Before the gorilla could make her way from around the counter to assist her girlfriend, I hopped over it and smacked her upside her head with the handle of my .380 pistol. *Bam!* "Bitch! Let's get it in!" I hollered.

She stumbled back into the potato chip rack, causing the rack to hit the floor with a loud crash. But, that didn't keep her down. Her big ass jumped up, blood seeping from the gash in her forehead. "You skinny bitch! I'mma kill you."

"Holy shit!" I searched around for an escape route. I didn't want her big ass sitting on me, crushing me like an ant. In an attempt to run past her, she pulled me by my shirt, and wrapped me into a bear hug.

"Die, you skinny bitch! Die!" She squeezed me so tight, I damn near pissed on myself.

I tried to flip the safety of my gun so I could buss this big bitch, but she managed to squeeze me harder, making it nearly impossible. I felt her bite me on the head as if she were a bear or something. That shit hurt so bad, I screamed. "Arrgh, bitch! Why you bitin' me like a lil' kid? Let me go, and fight me like a woman!"

Bam! Jennifer swung a metal pan that made contact with the gorilla's face. She fell through the glass cooler, where the soda pops were kept. Glass shattered all over the floor as sodas fell to the ground. Jennifer reached into the cooler and grabbed her by her nappy micro braids, slamming her knee into her face, before throwing her to the ground. "You silly bitch! Get the fuck off my cousin!"

I was so impressed, all I could do was kick the big bitch in her rib cage, causing her to flip over onto her back, then I straddled her, smacking her across the face with the pistol. "You dumb bitch! Where the safe at?"

Her face was covered in blood and remnants of the glass from the cooler could be spotted in her skin. Her eyes rolled in the back of her head, and she let out a few grunts. I could tell her body was going limp. I smacked her with the gun again, using more force than I had before, forcing her to slightly sit upright. "Where's the safe at?" I cocked my .380. "I'm not gon' say it again!"

"It's in the back, in the manager's office. Please! I don't know the combination though, only Ke-Ke do," she whimpered, blood running out of her mouth in globs.

"Who the fuck is Ke-Ke, bitch?" I glared at her, ready to blow her shit back. I was still salty about the fact that the fat bitch had bit me on top of my head, so I definitely wanted to knock some meat out of her taco.

I could see the light-skinned girl was struggling to get up. Jennifer hopped over the counter, aiming her .9 millimeter at her face. "I should murder you for thinkin' it was sweet. You have any idea what we've been through in life?" she asked, lowering her eyes into slits.

"Ke-Ke!" the gorilla yelled, as I tried to force my gun into her mouth. I had already knocked out her teeth, but everything in me wanted to blow her head off. "Ke-Ke, give them the money out the safe or they gon' kill us!" Shirley screamed.

Jennifer pushed Ke-Ke in the back so hard, she fell on the floor onto her knees. She started crying like a big ass baby, and that shit made me laugh.

"Bitch, now you wanna cry and shit! Where was all that emotional shit when you was actin' all tough? Now we done got all in that ass and yo true nature comin' to the forefront, huh?" I teased.

"Take me to the safe! Now!" Jennifer hollered, flipping her long hair over her shoulders. She had a menacing look on her face. A look I'd never seen before. It scared me and made me proud at the same time.

Ke-Ke got to her feet and nodded. "Look, I ain't go to the bank yesterday, so it's a nice amount in there. Y'all can have the money, just please don't hurt me or my woman."

Jennifer kicked her in the ass. "Bitch, let's go! You ain't in no position to be negotiatin' shit! Take us to the money. That's all you worry about."

I grabbed a handful of the gorilla's hair and sat on her back. "Bitch, act like you my horsey and giddy up. Follow them while I ride yo ass like a big ass mare." With that, I rode her back to the office, and once there, I leaned down and bit that bitch on her head in the same spot she had bit me in.

"Arrggghhh! Shit! The fuck is yo problem?"

"Yeah, that shit don't feel so good, do it?" I asked, spitting into the sink located in the office, before running the hot water. The bitch had so much dandruff in her hair, it tasted like sweaty pancake batter. I damn near threw up.

Jennifer held Ke-Ke by the throat, with her gun pressed into her right eye. "Bitch, if you try anything funny, I'm gon' blow yo shit right out. Just open the safe and put all the money in that Subway bag right there," she said, pointing to a white plastic bag that was on the desk. "You hear me?"

"I ain't gon' say nothin' either. I gotta take care of my mother, 'cuz she real sick. Please don't kill me, 'cuz I'm all she got." Shirley coughed up blood as she spoke up.
Jennifer threw Ke-Ke to the floor in front of the safe. "You broads got all this shit goin' on, but y'all in this mafucka runnin' y'all mouths like a drive-by shooter? Now we 'spose to feel sorry for y'all asses? Open the safe!"

I didn't feel shit for them. Far as I was concerned, fuck them, her sister's kids, the gorilla's momma, and the whole nine yards. Had we been some weak bitches, them hoes would've whooped our ass and called it a day.

Ke-Ke popped the safe open almost immediately. I dropped down and dug out the money bags they had inside of them. They felt kind of heavy, but I knew it couldn't have been major money in them.

Jennifer stood up with her gun directed at Ke-Ke. "Do you have any last words, bitch?"

"Yeah, and you say your last words, too." I looked at the gorilla.

They both dropped to their knees, hugging one another, crying like two big ass kindergarteners. I couldn't believe these were the same two females that had been talking all that tough shit.

"Please don't kill us. Please, please!" Ke-Ke cried, with so much snot coming out of her nose. It went right into her mouth and she kept on swallowing, like it was the most normal thing in the world. That bitch started to make me sick to my stomach. "Look, ain't no sense in cryin'. Y'all made y'all bed, now lie in it, 'cuz…"

Boom! Boom! Boom! "Fuck these hoes." *Boom! Boom! Boom!* Jennifer released bullet after bullet into their faces, causing blood to splash across the room.

Ghost

Chapter 15
J.T.

When I opened my eyes, the first thing I saw was Jennifer lean in and kiss Lil' Momma on the lips. I thought Lil' Momma was going to snap her head backward, but she leaned further into the kiss, moaning loudly. Her hand went under Jennifer's tank top and I watched it move around, until Jennifer threw her head backward and moaned. "Damn, lil' cuz, you makin' me wet as hell right now."

I wanted to get up and attack both of they asses, but I didn't want to interrupt what they had going on. Both of them were fine as hell in their own way. So, I wanted to see them get it in like the animals I knew they were.

Jennifer laid on her back and Lil' Momma got on top of her. Straddling her, she leaned down and sucked all over her lips loudly. "I love you, Jennifer. You always do your best to protect me. I love these soft ass lips too," she said, licking them and sucking them into her mouth.

"Uhh-mm," Jennifer moaned, helping Lil' Momma out of her wife beater. Her round, perfect lil' titties bounced, before Jennifer pulled on the nipple with her fingers, after licking them first.

Lil' Momma then moaned, and slid her hand into Jennifer's tight shorts. Jennifer opened her legs wide as her hands squeezed Lil' Momma's titties. She ran her thumbs across her nipples, until Lil' Momma crawled backward, pulling Jennifer shorts down and off her ankles. Then, she attacked her pussy through the panties, while Jennifer pulled them up and further into her pussy crack.

"Eat me, Lil' Momma! Eat my pussy now! I love you so fuckin' much!" she moaned.

Lil' Momma yanked her panties down, baring her bald yellow pussy. She spread the lips of her sex with her fingers before her head disappeared. All I could hear was loud slurping noises and Jennifer moaning like she was having the time of her life. Her legs were spread so wide, it looked like she was hitting the splits.

"Uhh-mmm, shit, Lil' Momma! It's so good! I'm comin' alreadeeeee!" she screamed, grabbing Lil' Momma's head and pulling her face into her lap.

Lil' Momma's head was going from side to side. The slurping sounds got louder, and she even started to growl like an angry wolf.

When Jennifer pulled her up and on top of her, they started tonguing each other down, while Jennifer rubbed all over her ass. I lost it. I pulled my boxers down and off. My dick was already standing out in front of me like a baseball bat. I knelt down behind Lil' Momma and yanked her pink Burberry skirt up, ripped her laced Burberry panties off of her and slammed my dick into her tight and wet oozing pussy, causing her to shriek.

"Aww! Shit, daddy! Fuck yo baby girl like only you can. Please!" she growled through clenched teeth.

I grabbed her hips and slammed her into me digging my dick deeply into her. At the same time, I watched Jennifer finger fuck herself while she popped her C-cup titties out. Her brown nipples stood out damn near an inch, it looked like. She ran her tongue across her pretty lips and opened her legs wide. Just watching her fingers running in and out of her pussy made me punish Lil' Momma. She already had some bomb ass pussy, but the fact that Jennifer was in the room watching me fuck her cousin, while she played with her pussy, added to the equation.

"Fuck me, daddy! Ohh, shit, I love you, J.T. You my daddy! Can't nobody do me like you do meee!" she hollered. Then, I felt her walls vibrating all around my dick. Her pussy started squirting like she always did when she came, and that made me speed up the pace like a maniac.

Jennifer came over and put her face right under Lil' Momma's stomach. She put her fingers into the gap where my dick went in and out of her, collected our juices, and sucked them from her fingers. "Lil' Momma, you gotta let me fuck him next. Please! I'm a part of this family too. I gotta get some of that pipe." She kissed my balls and sucked on my thighs.

Her breath felt hot and it turned me on. I reached across her back and squeezed her big ass booty, slapping it before trailing my finger down to her asshole and sliding it in.

She arched her back and let out a long moan. Then, she spread her thick thighs, turned around and bussed her pussy open right in Lil' Momma's face. She laid her head on the floor, reached under herself and opened her lips wide.

I slammed into Lil' Momma with so much force, I felt my abs locking up. The feel of her pussy seemed to be getting hotter and wetter. I smacked her super hard on the ass, then pushed my dick as deep in her as it would go, letting my seed fly.

"Huhh-unnn, unnhh! I feel you, daddy. Come in mee! Yesss! Aww, shit, dadddeeee!" She started shaking so much, it felt like she was having a seizure. She fell to the floor on her stomach, causing my dick to slide out of her. It stood up like an oiled, oversized, brown cucumber with a million veins running through it.

As soon as I popped it out, Jennifer grabbed it in her hand. She stroked it up and down a few times before sucking the head into her mouth. I felt her running her tongue across it, then she popped it back out, making a loud smacking noise that drove me crazy.

"Lil' Momma, please let me hop on this dick, Cousin. Please, I'll do anything," she begged, sliding two fingers into herself.

Lil' Momma flipped onto her back and spread her thighs wide. "Go ahead. You gotta feel how he be puttin' it down. I ain't tripping about y'all fucking, just as long as it don't happen behind my back. Go!"

Jennifer didn't waste no time at all. She tackled me to the floor, then grabbed my pole, running it up and down her crease until he found the hole. "Uh-unn, J.T!" she moaned, sliding all the way backward onto it.

I reached around her and took ahold of that big ass booty. It felt so round and soft. I used it to lift her up and slammed her down on my dick. Her pussy was just as wet and tight as Lil' Momma's, only difference was the smell. They both had their own individual scents, but nevertheless, it had me feeling some type of way.

Lil' Momma crawled behind Jennifer and started sucking all over her thick ass cheeks. I could hear the sounds of her lips on her ass. "Yeah, you like how he fucking that pussy up, don't you, Jenn? That mafucka all in yo stomach, ain't it?" Lil' Momma bit into her back.

"Uhnn-shit, yes! It feels so good. Dammit, it feels so good! I'm coming already this dick got me fuckin', ahhh!" She leaned her head back, slamming her crotch into mine. I could feel her pussy spitting while I sucked all over her big titties. Her hard nipples grazed against my lips and my nose. Her lil' body was on fire.

She sat all the way up on my dick, and planted a kiss on my lips. Lil' Momma came repeatedly and we all continued to do the most while I long-stroked Jennifer, until I came deep within her. When it was all said and done, we laid sprawled out on the floor, kissing and sucking all over one another.

***

"What the fuck you mean, y'all had to body two bitches to get this money?" I asked, dumping the bags out on the floor and running my Jordan's through the pile of cash. Just by eyeing it, I could tell that it couldn't have been more than fifteen G's. Personally, I'd kill one mafucka for fifteen G's, but two? But, that wasn't the point. The point was that they had bussed a move without me, and anything could have gone wrong. It seemed like there was a million police rolling around the neighborhood.

"It didn't even start out like that though. Them bitches was 'bout to jump on Lil' Momma and I wasn't 'bout to let that shit fly. So, it started out with us just whoopin' they ass, but then I figured, why not make the setback beneficial?" Jennifer said, sticking a chopstick in her Chinese food.

"Yeah, them hoes was twice as big as us. One bitch actually locked the door of the store, before they got on some gangsta shit that cost them their lives. You would have done the same thing, so kiss my ass if you mad, 'cause I ain't tryna hear it." Lil' Momma scooped up the barbeque chicken with her fork, dumping it into her mouth.

"Lil' Momma, you tryin' me right now, fa'real. Don't think I won't spank yo lil' ass, 'cuz I will. I'm head of this mafuckin' family, so ya betta get yo shit together," I said, glaring at her lil' fine, evil ass. Sometimes, she did and said shit that made me want to fuck her up. I would discipline her in a minute, too.

She lowered her head. "I'm sorry, baby, but all I'm sayin' is them hoes tried to kill us in that store. Had we not bodied them, then they would be on the run and we would be the dead bodies. I know you wouldn't want that. Right?" She gave me that sexy, adorable look that made me put my G-card away.

"You already know I wouldn't want that. I'd kill every mafucka in Vegas over y'all." I frowned. "Man, I just hope y'all were smart, 'cuz they finna be all over that crime scene. We gotta get the fuck outta here by the end of the week. I got one more caper to pull out here and then we gone." I smacked Lil' Momma on the ass. "Next time, y'all tell me right away when y'all buss a move like this, that way I know what's goin' on and I'll know how to maneuver. This ski mask shit come wit strategy. We just can't be knockin mafuckas' heads off just to be doin' it. Y'all understand?"

They both nodded, then went back to eating. I couldn't do shit but laugh, watching Lil' Momma rub her ass where I slapped it.

***

"I hear you fuckin' with some Greek nigga now that be cashin' you out and everything. Word around town is that you and Kelly is knee deep in the game," I said, walking alongside Veronica on the beach. She had hit me up two days after the Subway incident with Lil' Momma and Jennifer, and basically begged me to meet her at the Monona Grove Beach, outside of Las Vegas.

It was eight in the morning and she wanted to walk along the water with our bare feet. It didn't bother me none, because I needed to pick her brain. I knew she was a very emotional woman.

"I really don't wanna talk about business today. I've been talkin' about it every day for the last five years. I just wanna catch up with you. I've really missed you, J.T. My love for you ain't changed." She wrapped her arm around my waist

and laid her head on my shoulder. She smelled like Chanel N°
5. I knew that to be her favorite perfume, even as a kid.

"I see you still smell the same, even though you havin'
major money now. I guess a part of you wanted to maintain
that little innocence that was always sexy to me." I kissed her
on the cheek, then squeezed that big ass booty.

Veronica was caramel-skinned with long, curly hair. She
resembled a young version of Stacey Dash, but was strapped
with it. She had on a tight ass Gucci dress that hugged her so
tight, it kept rising every time she took a step. She had to keep
on pulling it down, and more than once it wound up around
her waist, exposing her light blue, laced panties.

She lifted her head and kissed me on the cheek. "I wish I
were still an innocent little girl. Times were much simpler
back then. Now, I'm so corrupt, I don't know what to do with
myself," she said, squeezing my hand.

Hearing that made my antennas perk up. I sensed
something was wrong, I could feel it radiating from her body.
I pulled her closer to me as the sand squished between my
toes. "Baby, what's the matter?" I turned her around so that
she was facing me, kissing her on the forehead.

She lowered her head, and blinked back tears. "I don't
know, J.T. I don't wanna say. I haven't seen you in so long
and the last thing I wanna do is get you involved in some
bullshit." She was crying fully now, sniffing snot back into
her nose. She was one of the few females I had ever seen
actually look good while they cried. Not many women could
pull that off. Even though I emotionally didn't feel shit for her,
I had to play my role because I smelled money all over this
bitch.

I rubbed her chin and kissed her on the forehead. "Baby,
you can tell me anything. Ain't shit changed between us. I still
got yo back against all odds. We been deeply rooted ever since

we were kids and that ain't never supposed to change." I hugged her, then made her take a step back.

"Now, tell me what's wrong, before I spank that big ass of yours."

She slowly looked up to me and smiled weakly. "J.T., I'm not happy with this man I'm with. I mean, he gives me everything I want, and I travel all over the world, but there's no love there. The sex sucks, and he beats on me weekly for every little thing. I am tired of being his punching bag. I'm tired of being his captive slave. I want to break free and I need some good dick in my life." She groaned, cuffing my penis through my shorts. "I miss this right here." She took her hand and slid it all the way into my shorts until she wrapped my dick in her little hand.

"So, baby, what are you sayin' to me, 'cuz you know how I get down? Are you hintin' that you want me to body this nigga so you can break free? I mean, what's your purpose for callin' me out here to this beach early in the mornin'?" I watched the water crash into the big rocks, off into the distance. About six seagulls flew overhead, screeching loudly.

The wind blew lightly across my face, and the sand felt warm in between my toes and under my feet. I felt her rubbing her thumb across my dick head, causing him to rise to the point he was out of my waistband. I had visions of fucking this bitch right here on the beach. She was a lunatic for that anal shit, and if it meant I could possibly put my crew up on some serious cash, then I was all for it.

"No, baby. I don't want you to kill him. Well actually, I do, but not until we hit his pockets in a major way. I'm talking millions, all in cash spread out in different locations that only I have the current knowledge of, well, besides him. I have all of his blueprints. I know what each person working for him has, and how much. My proposal to you would be for you to knock off as many of his spots as possible. That way it will bleed him monetarily. Money and product is the only power that he has. If we can bleed him until he's broke, then he will lose his power, and then you can kill him and I can be free."

I frowned. "All that shit sounds good, but what's in it for me? I mean, you my girl and everything, and I'd anything for you, but there still has to be an incentive for me to get at this mafucka."

"Seventy percent." She rubbed my chest with both of her hands. "Seventy percent of everything you cop you can keep. I'll give you the ins and outs of everything. All you have to do is knock off the locations that I give you, at the times that I give you and there shouldn't be any problems. I mean, you aren't afraid to get your hands bloody, right?" She raised an eyebrow and looked at me from the side of her face.

I gave her a look that told her to quit playing with me, by curling up my lip and frowning. "As long as them numbers right, I don't give a fuck whose blood I gotta wash my hands in. You just make sure you handle your end and I'll take care of mine, because I'm trusting you on this. I don't usually put my faith in nobody."

I really didn't trust her more than one percent. The way I saw shit was, this Boris mafucka was already spoiling her ass to the max and she still wasn't happy. I felt like she was greedy and had that snake shit in her blood. She was probably a little bit of a control freak, too. But, the fact that she was crossing a man that was going all out of his way for her, made me know I had to play this bitch real close, even though we had grown up together.

She wrapped her arms around my waist, stood on her tippy toes and kissed my lips. "Baby, I got you. The way I'mma set shit up, his organization ain't even gonna see it comin' until it's much too late."

"Yeah ma, I'mma hold you to it."

Chapter 16
Lil' Momma

I was already sweating like a mafucka by the time I slid my ski mask over my face. It was a hundred and ten degrees outside and the humidity was through the roof. I had sweat pouring all down my back, and my thighs were sticking to one another. I felt icky but at the same time, my heart was beating so fast, it was making it hard for me to calm down.

I looked over at Jennifer as she slid her black mask over her face and slammed the long clip into her TEC-9. She nodded at me and I returned her nod. We were in the alley behind Luigi's Pizza, about to knock off the first establishment J.T. had okayed for us to buss down by ourselves. We had spent three days going over the move. He had even supplied us with pictures of the interior of the restaurant and we knew exactly where we were supposed to go and hit. I was amped up because I was ready to blast some shit, and I was proud that J.T. trusted us enough to buss moves on our own. That said a lot about how he felt about us.

I took another deep breath and crouched low to the ground. It was three pm and I was just worried about witnesses or innocent bystanders. I didn't want to kill more people than I had to, but if it came down to that, then so be it.

"Girl, you all right over there?" Jennifer asked, crouching down beside me as we ducked down behind the big garbage can behind the establishment. She adjusted her mask on her face, then wiped the sweat out of her eyes.

I nodded. "I'm good, let's go in here and hit that safe. Remember, J.T. said we gotta locate the fat Italian bitch with the mustache. She got the combo. And we wet any mafucka that look like they on bullshit."

Jennifer nodded. "I already know and I'm ready. Let's go!" She took off running toward the back of the restaurant, where there was a screen door that led directly into the kitchen. As soon as she opened the door, there was a man wearing a white apron, with his hair slicked back into a ponytail. Jennifer ran right up to him and slammed the clip and handle of her TEC-9 right into his forehead. He fell backward, and his head hit the side of the counter before he fell down, knocked out cold.

I ran in behind her and pointed my MAK-90 at a heavyset man that looked like he ate way more pizzas then he sold. When he saw me in the mask, he threw his hands into the air and dropped down to his knees. "A-please don't-a shoot me," he said, in a thick Italian accent.

I took his head and slammed it into the metal cabinet behind him, then slammed the butt of my gun into the back of his head. He fell to the floor face down, knocked out cold. I kicked his punk ass in the ribs a few times to flip him over, until he wound up under the sink out of sight. Jennifer rolled the other man into the spice cabinet and closed the door.

Lucky for us, the kitchen was all the way in the back of the restaurant and out of sight from the customers. In order to get into it, you had to enter through a swinging door. This was the same door I peeked out of just to see what I could see.

To the left, I saw a younger Italian female standing behind the cash register. She was taking the order of a customer, an old man that kept himself up by leaning on a cane. With the exception of him, there was not another customer in sight. Looking to my right, I saw what had to be the older fat Italian woman J.T. was talking about. I could make out her mustache even from where I stood and that got my heart to beating fast once again. I slowly stepped back and allowed the door to close.

Jennifer was standing right behind me with her eyes wide open. "Who's all out there? Do you see the bitch he was talking about?" she asked, looking me up and down.

I nodded. "Yeah, that bitch's sitting right outside the door to our right. It's one customer out there, and then some teenage girls I say we go out here and handle business and get this job over with. You go left and..."

Before I could finish what I was saying, the door swung inward and hit me in the forehead, knocking me on my ass. I dropped my gun and everything and shit got blurry.

"Bitch!" I heard Jennifer's voice and then I heard a whole bunch of sounds. It sounded like something was being beat over and over again. I tried to shake the cobwebs out of my head.

I looked up in time to see Jennifer straddling the girl and beating her over the head with a skillet repeatedly. Her gun was on the side of her and she was working her over like crazy.

Shaking my head super hard, I regained my composure, picked up my MAK-90 and bussed through the swinging door running to my right where the fat lady with the mustache was sitting. As soon as she saw me, she threw her hands into the air and damn near fell off her stool. She had to catch herself by placing one hand on the counter for leverage.

"Bitch, get the fuck up and come with me!" I said, grabbing a handful of her hair and yanking her off of the stool roughly. She fell straight to her knees and I pulled her up.

"Hey, I'll give you whatever you want, just don't hurt me or my granddaughter. The safe is in my office. I'll take you to it. I won't give you any problems, just take the money and go!" she said with her neck bent awkwardly, because I had a fistful of her hair.

I handled her rough, snatching her up as I watched Jennifer make the old man lie on his stomach, while she closed and locked the front door of the restaurant, flipping the open sign around to closed.

"Let's go!" I pushed the mustached lady in the back so hard that she flew through the swinging door and onto her knees. She landed right in a pool of blood and started to scream.

"Ahhhh! Oh my God, Suri! What have you done to my granddaughter!" She crawled to her and cradled her into her arms.

The girls head was bashed in. Her eyes wide open and crossed. Her face was covered in blood, yet her stomach moved in and out, showing signs that she was alive. She started to shake, and finally she blinked her eyes repeatedly.

I didn't know whether to snatch the old woman up, or to give her a few seconds to console her being granddaughter. Fortunately, Jennifer bussed through the door and made the decision for me. She smacked me upside the head and grabbed the old woman up by her hair.

"Bitch, time is of the essence! Take me to the safe right now or I'mma put a bullet in your head, and hers!"

"Ow! Okay!" the woman hollered as Jennifer manhandled her all the way back to the office. I could hear her threatening her along the way.

Meanwhile, the girl who was still lying on her back, tried to get up. There was lots of blood coming out of her mouth and she looked like she was in so much pain. For a brief second, I felt sorry for her because I knew that she was suffering. Being in the wrong place at the wrong time had gotten her life taken.

I looked around the kitchen until I found a big, ridged steak knife. Once I got it, I knelt down by the girl, and pulled her up by her hair roughly to expose her neck. I took the blade and dragged it from one side of her neck all the way to the other, killing her and saving her from the intense torture and pain she was going through. I felt like I was doing a good deed. Had I been suffering the way she was, I would want someone to slice my throat the way I had done hers.

I dropped her head and watched it bounce off the floor like a basketball, then I dragged her under the sink, along with our other victim before running into the back office. I got there just in time to see the old woman jump on Jennifer's back and they fell to the floor. I saw she had her arm wrapped around Jennifer's neck with a shiny blade in her hand.

"Ya keep struggling, girl, and I'll cut ya from ear to ear. I swear I will, with no remorse for the killing."

Jennifer laid out flat on her back with her arms out at her side, while the old woman squatted down on the side of her.

Bam! "You punk ass bitch! Get the fuck off of her!" I said, slamming the laptop computer that sat on the desk over her head.

She fell to her side knocked out cold. The blade flew from her hand and was swallowed up under the desk. Jennifer jumped up, holding her neck. I could see a drop of blood pool down into her black shirt, from where the old woman had cut her.

"That bitch tried to kill me," she said, looking down on the old lady with the mustache. She took her foot and kicked her so hard in the ribs, she fell onto the desk.

I looked over at the safe and saw that it was wide open. Jennifer must have been on her way to throwing the money in a garbage bag, because there was one on the side of the safe, and money all over the floor in front of it. I went to get it and started to load the bag up. I couldn't believe the stacks and stacks of cash the safe had in it. Another thing that shocked me was the silver-packaged bricks inside. I knew it had to be dope in them, so I threw them in the bag with all of the money.

"Awright, let's go, girl!" I said to Jennifer.

She was still looking down on the woman with hate in her eyes. Finally, she cocked her TEC-9 and stomped the woman in the stomach. "Bitch!" *Bop! Bop! Bop!*

The woman's body leaped off of the floor as the bullets ate at her flesh. I saw a huge pool of blood flooded the small office before we ran out of there.

Chapter 17
Jennifer

"Fuck, girl! Punch that shit! Get us out of here!" I said, stabbing a hole into the airbag that deployed when Lil' Momma crashed into two garbage cans in the middle of the alley. As soon as we hit them, two people riding all-black Ducati's appeared in the alley with machine guns. *Bocka! Bocka! Bocka! Chhhsshh!* Our back windows shattered, and that's when Lil' Momma crashed into the garbage cans. My heart was beating so fast, I thought I was going to pass out.

"Shit! Shit! Shit! Where did they come from?" she screamed, throwing the car into reverse and slamming on the gas taking us backwards at sixty miles an hour down the narrow alley.

We rolled back past the restaurant and I got a chill that ran down my spine. We had left that joint filled up with bodies. I could only imagine it was the reason we had two masked people on motorcycles, chasing us with heavy artillery. *Bocka! Bocka! Bocka!* They rained shots, and I had to duck down in my seat. I was praying none of their bullets would go through our seats. I had seen that happen on a movie before and I was starting to panic. I wondered if J.T. knew we had been taking this much heat

Errrrrh! Our car screeched as Lil' Momma slammed on the brakes and turned the wheels, so the car could face in the direction of the residential street. Once the car straightened out, she stepped on the gas again and the car jerked forward, before speeding through the neighborhood.

Bocka! Bocka! Bocka! Bocka! Errrr-onnn! One of the drivers of the Ducati sped up alongside of the car on Lil'

Momma's side and got ready to aim the machine gun directly at her.

I leaned across her lap. *Boom! Boom! Boom! Boom!* Fucking bussin' my gun with my tongue out. The bullets smacked into his or her chest. I couldn't tell because they wore a helmet and I'd knocked them off of their bike. The rider flew on top of a car before flying to the sidewalk, while the Ducati crashed into a car and exploded.

"Ahhhhhh! Good lookin', Cousin! I thought that muthafucka had me dead to the world. I owe you my life!" Lil' Momma hollered. She made a hard left and flew down another alley, and came out onto another deserted street.

I looked over our shoulder, trying to locate the other bike, but it was nowhere in sight. I exhaled loudly and sat back in my seat. I couldn't wait until we were back with J.T. I needed to hug him. I needed to feel secure. I needed to tell him how close me and Lil' Momma had been to actual death. I closed my eyes to say a silent prayer as Lil' Momma turned onto the expressway.

Boom! My neck snapped forward as we were crashed into from behind. I opened my eyes and turned around to see a black Lincoln Navigator with tinted windows barreling down on our car. It sped up again and crashed into the bumper, knocking me forward and the car swerved, clipping another one.

"What the fuck is going on?" Lil' Momma hollered. She stepped on the gas and started to zigzag through traffic.

Errrrr-onnn! Another Ducati pulled up on the side of my window and the driver extended his arm, with an Uzi in his hand. *Thaat! Thaat! Thaat! Thaat!*

My windows shattered, and I heard the bullets slamming into the door. I ducked down low in my seat to get out the way of the gunfire. "Hit his ass, Lil' Momma!" I demanded. "Hit his ass before he kills us!"

Errrrr! Whoom! The car jerked, and I felt her make impact, slamming into the Ducati. The bike wobbled and crashed into the back of another car, sending the rider flying into the sky. He landed in front of the car and it rolled over him.

I looked over at Lil' Momma and I wanted to start crying, because her right arm was covered in blood. "Oh my God, Lil' Momma! Baby, where are you hit?" I screamed, about to go into panic mode.

She stepped on the gas and weaved into the exit lane, flying at seventy miles an hour onto the ramp. "That fuck nigga shot me in the shoulder and it's hurting like hell. I'm trying my best not to think about the pain, because J.T. said that's what you're 'spose to do. You're 'spose to pretend that it never happened."

I watched the blood spurt out of her shoulder and run down her arm. Looking behind us, the Navigator was about four cars back. It had taken the exit, just as we had. I didn't know who was in the truck or why they were after us, but one thing I did figure out was they were definitely out to kill us. "Lil' Momma, you gotta lose them. You gotta lose them, so I can get behind the wheel and get you to a hospital. You're losing a lot of blood right now." I said, placing my hand over the hole in her arm. Blood oozed through my fingers. It felt like hot, sticky syrup.

"Okay, Jenn. I know what I gotta do, Cousin, but I'm gettin' dizzy." She blinked her eyes a few times and shook her head really hard.

I was starting to panic as she turned onto a side street so fast, the car nearly flipped over. It spun on two wheels before slamming back down on all fours. She stepped on the gas and flew down the street until we got to the end of the block, where she slammed on the brakes to respect the stop sign. As soon as she did, she passed out with her face in the steering wheel.

Beeeeeppppp! The constant sound of the car horn blared, until I pulled her up and slowly placed her in the passenger seat, snapping the seatbelt across her. I climbed into the driver's seat, threw the car in drive and *errrrr-uhh!* I sped away from the curb with the tires spinning.

I got about three blocks down, when I stopped at another stop sign, only pausing briefly. I stepped on the gas prepared to drive out into the intersection when *bam!* The sound of metal smashing and crunching could be heard as our car was hit so hard, it spun in a circle twice before coming to a halt in the middle of the street.

My head slammed into the steering wheel and it busted open my left eye immediately. My head bounced off the steering wheel and jerked backward, forcing me back into my seat. Somehow, across from me, Lil' Momma had landed on the floor of the passenger seat crunched into a ball.

I heard the sound of cars slamming on their brakes and then car doors slamming. I could hear police sirens off in the distance. I was afraid to open my eyes, afraid to face what our fate was about to become.

Chapter 18
J.T.

"I ain't playing no muthafuckin' games wit you, ma nigga. This shit is serious business," I said, as I finished duct taping the last bitch nigga to the chair.

Me and Rip had waited until the cocaine party was damn near finished, before Veronica buzzed us into the gate. With ski masks, we bussed through the pool house door with guns out. There was only four men left at the round glass table and they were taking turns, snorting up healthy lines of powdered cocaine from what seemed like two kilos on the table.

Kelly and Boris were two of the four men. One was her brother and the other, her fiancé. She had already said that she didn't want either one of them killed, unless I really had to. Due to the fact that Kelly had been beefing with my cousin ever since we were kids, I was hoping that I would have to knock his head off.

As soon as we bussed through the glass door with a loud *wham,* glass went flying everywhere. The doors were so weak, the one kick damn near had them hanging on by the hinges. I ran right over to the table and grabbed Boris by his ponytail, yanking him from the seat roughly, with my MAK-90 pressed so hard into his temple, it broke the skin. "Muthafucka, you gon' take me upstairs to the safe and you gon' empty it out or I'm gon' splattered your brains all on these marbled floors," I hissed through clenched teeth.

He threw his arms into the air. His face was covered with the powdered cocaine. It looked like he'd been eating powdered donuts face-first all day long. "Listen, man, you're making a really huge mistake. You'll never get away with this. I'd advise you to go out the way you came, and I'll forget this ever happened," he said, scrunching up his face with hatred.

Rip went up to the table and smacked Kelly so hard with his Calico gun, he fell backward out of the chair and crashed to the floor. At the same time, he pointed a MAK-11 at the other two remaining men. "Everybody get on the ground and lay on yo muthafuckin' faces! Now!"

Kelly slowly turned over to follow his directives. His face was covered in blood and mucous. "You mafuckas will never get away with this. You're committin' suicide. Both of you."

The other two older men laid on their stomachs without a word. I sensed they were hip to the game and all they cared about was escaping with their lives intact. Both were well-dressed in expensive Gucci linens. I figured they had to have been some kind of power players in Boris' grand scheme of things.

I watched Rip grab Kelly up, then put his hand around his neck until he walked him backward and slammed him into the wall hard. "You bitch ass nigga! You always got something to say, like you the hardest nigga in the world. Before it's all said and done, I'mma punch your brains outta yo skull, cuz."

Boris jerked his head. "Let my hair g,o you son of a bitch! If you really want to commit suicide like this, then who am I to stop you? You want the fuckin' money? I'll get you your fuckin' money! Take me upstairs, but let my hair go!" Once again, he tried to jerk his head away from me.

In one swift motion I picked him up, and then dumped him on his head. He hit the marbled floor hard. Then I knelt down and grabbed a fistful of his hair and put my face right next to his. "I don't give a fuck how bad you think you is, white boy, don't none of that shit fly wit me. Now, you gon' get yo punk ass up and we gon' go get this money. You make one more demand and I'm gon' turn your Greek ass into a gyro! You understandin' me right now?"

He gave me a look that said he wanted to kill me in cold blood. His eyelids lowered into slits, and then he curled his upper lip. "Yez, I hear you loud and clear. Let me show you where everything is." He started to climb to his feet.

I yanked him upward and wrapped my arm around his throat from the back, putting MAK-90 to the back of his head ready to pull the trigger if I had to. I didn't give a fuck about him or nobody else in that house, and that included my cousin to a certain extent. My mindset was on getting every piece of money in that house, and then bouncing back to my girls. I was worried about them, and hoped that they were able to handle their mission the right ski mask way. I had faith in them, but that didn't stop me from second guessing everything. I felt like a father that had given his child the keys to his whip for the first time. Even though you knew they were ready to drive, you still worried about them every single second that car was not in the driveway.

Boris led me up the spiral staircase Veronica had already described to me. I knew once we got to the top landing, we were supposed to go straight down the long hallway, until we came to the master bedroom door. She said it was a double door that opened inward. I was waiting for him to try and take me to any other room in the upstairs part of the mansion, and I was gon' make him pay for it. But, he didn't. he led me all the way to the door and opened it.

The first thing I saw was a big bed with Louis Vuitton blankets. The nightstands had L.V. on each one of them, and even the lampshades were custom-made in Louis Vuitton. I figured Boris had some form of an obsession with the designer, because I had seen a lot of Louis Vuitton all over the house. Even looking out of the bedroom window, I could see straight downward into the big pool in the backyard. That water was clear and blue as mouthwash. Directly at the bottom of the pool, I could see the initials L.V.

When we got into the room, I slung Boris into it roughly and he fell on the floor looking up to me. I kept my weapon aimed at him while I went to the right-side night table and knocked it over and kicked it out of the way. I knew the safe was supposed to be under it, after you peeled the carpet back.

"Aiight, nigga, pull that carpet back and pull that mafucka up. I ain't got no time for these games. Go!" I said, grabbing his hair and pulling him in the direction of where the safe was supposed to be located.

He fell onto his stomach, and then crawled the rest of the way. He peeled back the carpet, crawling backward until I saw a digital green face light up, and buttons on the side of the screen. It looked almost like an ATM machine. He reached to press the buttons, and then stopped. "Before I do this, how do you know so much about me?" he frowned. "You come into my home and you manhandle me and my friends. Then, you come in here, knowing exactly where my safe is, as if somebody has given you blueprints on me. Tell who it is and fuck this robbery. I'll make you a very rich man." He gave me a look that said he was serious.

I leaned down and backhanded him so hard that he flew against the side of the bed. Then I snatch him up by his hair and yanked his head backward nearly snapping his neck. "Open that safe right now or I'm gon' kill you," I growled, slinging him back on top of it.

I held the gun to the back of his head. He started to punch in the code, mumbling under his breath. Every time he punched one of the buttons, they beeped. Finally, the beeping stopped, and he took his hand and placed it on the screen. The screen went from black to all green and it started to flash for about three seconds. "System disarmed." *Beep, beep cussshhh!* The large face of the safe popped open. It was the size of a mini refrigerator.

As soon as it did, he opened the door all the way, and all I could see was stacks and stacks of money, as if they had been stuffed inside of it. Grabbing him by his ponytail, I dragged him away from the safe and wrapped my arm around his neck. We fell to the floor with me squeezing underneath his jawbone with all of my might. Putting him into the sleeper hold, applying massive pressure to his jaw and chin, I could hear the bones popping in them.

He struggled against me at first, trying to slap at my forearm and twist his body this way and that way. But, there was nothing he could do, because I refused to let him go until he laid before me limp. I slammed my fist into his stomach, knocking the wind out of him and tightened my hold until he quit moving. I held it a full minute longer and then released him.

I got up and fucked up the neatly-made bed. Taking two of the pillows, dumping them out of their pillowcases, I took the pillowcases and filling them with stack after stack of money. I packed them so fast I was sweating profusely under my hot ass ski mask. With every stack I put into the pillowcase, the smile on my face grew wider. I got to thinking about how me, Lil' Momma, and Jennifer would be able to flee to Miami, living comfortably for a minute.

I would have my mother snatched up and placed in rehab as soon as I figured out that situation. I could only imagine the pigs were going crazy looking for us out in California, which meant that we had to travel as far East as possible. I was even thinking about leaving the country altogether, because it could only be a matter of time before we were tracked down some kind of way. Them people didn't play about murders or a mafucka trying to hurt they officers. Because of Looney and the shit with him, me and the girls were on the run for both offenses.

After I emptied the safe, I ran out of the room and down the spiral staircase. I went right back into the den where I had left Rip and the other three men. What I saw made me freeze in my tracks. Rip had the two older men face down on the marbled floor with a pool of blood under them. I could see that their throats had been cut wide open. The closer I got to them, the more I could make out the sadistic scene. It looked like both men's necks were open mouths. All I could do was shake my head.

Rip was just finishing duct taping Kelly to a chair. He got up when he saw me, reached and smacked the shit out of Kelly. I could hear him screaming through the tape. "I gotta kill this nigga, Cuz. He knows who I am, and he said my name in front of them other two mafia bosses out there. Ain't no other way, but first he gon' tell me where them birds at."

"Yo nigga, we gotta get a move on it though. I got the money from the safe, so body that nigga and let's bounce." I sat the filled pillowcases down. "Fuck!"

"What's good?" I noted he had a big ass hunting knife in his hand that was dripping with blood.

"I'll be back. Since you killin' everybody, I gotta go finish this mafucka upstairs, because I only put his ass to sleep. I thought we was gonna keep everything on the up and up."

He waved me off. "Hell, nawl! Go kill that nigga. Then we gotta hit Veronica's ass, because she gon' flip when she finds out her punk ass brother dead, even though I don't give a fuck." Before he even finished what he was saying to me, he squished the knife through the air and sliced Kelly across one cheek. Punched him with a closed fist, then sliced him again on the other cheek. "Bitch ass nigga, I ain't playin' wit you, you gon' tell me where them birds at, so me and my people can eat, cuz, or else it's gonna be painful until you die." He punched him repeatedly, this time so hard he fell out of the chair.

I helped him pick him back up and sit him onto it. I wanted to see exactly what he was going to do, because I never knew that he got downright mean. I thought he was strictly about that gunplay and didn't have that heinous shit in him. So, I wanted to watch every second of this. I slung the nigga back onto his chair and held him by the shoulder. Kelly was screaming behind the duct tape and I mean screaming loud. That shit had me smiling. I could only imagine how much pain he was in. I shook my head. It seemed like sooner or later, the life always caught up to bitch niggas and when it did, they rarely could handle it.

Rip took the point of the knife and poked it into Kelly's cheek and slowly broke it down his face. "Now nigga, once I take this duct tape off of your mouth, you gon' tell me where them birds at. Then, you gon' find some way to confirm that you tellin' me the truth, because if I detect that you are lyin', then we gon' have a big ass problem. You gettin' me, cuz?"

Kelly started moving around crazy in the chair as Rip drug the knife from his mouth all the way down to his neck. Blood poured out of the wound and dripped off of his face. I could see inside of his flesh and that shit got me excited.

Rip snatched the tape off of his mouth. "Speak, nigga, and make every muthafuckin' word count."

"Ahhh!" He smacked his lips together. "It's in the wall of my manager's office at the barbershop man. It's sixty keys of pure heroin. I swear to God, if you let me live, Rip, you can have every last one of them. And I got one and a half million in cash put up. You can have all that shit, just let me leave out this mafucka with my life. I'm scared to die, man. Please!" He started crying like a big-ass baby and that shit made me crack up.

I smacked the shit out of him so hard, I felt my wrist snap. "Shut that bitch shit up, nigga! You down here cryin' like you ain't know what you was gettin' yoself into when you stepped into the game. Ain't no mercy, bitch nigga. None!"

There were very few things worse than a crying grown man. I hated them type of niggaz. It wasn't the first time I had pulled a caper and the nigga that got caught up started sniveling and crying like a bitch, once I started tearing into his ass. That only made me go that much harder, before I eventually killed him by drowning his ass in the bathroom toilet.

Rip stabbed the knife into his jaw. "Ahhh! Shit! Why are you doing this to me? I said I'd give you everything I got! Just stop this shit!" He hollered

"Nigga, shut the fuck up, cuz! I don't like all that cryin' shit either, so the more you cry like a bitch, the more pain I'm gonna inflict on yo bitch ass. You wasn't doin' alla this cryin' and shit when you were givin' the orders for yo niggaz to kill my niggaz, but now all of a sudden, big bad Kelly cryin' foul ball. Nigga, please." He pulled the knife out of his face and turned to me. "Aye, Cuz, go get Boris' bitch ass. Let me finish handling this business wit him. By the time you get back, I'll be ready."

I nodded, laughed and smacked the shit out of Kelly one more time, knocking him out of his chair. Rip stomped him in the chest and straddled him. I could hear him yelping as I jogged up the spiral staircase. I didn't want to waste no time with Boris. I was gon' go right into the room, put the MAK to the back of his head and pull the trigger, knocking meat out of his taco.

We needed to get the fuck outta that house and on the road. I was already feeling some type of way because it was obvious Veronica had to be killed. I didn't trust her not to turn on me, especially after she found out that her brother had been murdered. There was no way I could sleep at night, knowing she was roaming around with all of this knowledge. I was supposed to meet up with her at Nobu at nine pm that night to fill her in on what had taken place. I planned on doing just that, but I would have Lil' Momma finish her off before the night was over with. I was sure my baby girl would have no problem doing that. That made me laugh a little bit.

I got back to the door of the master bedroom where I had left Boris and opened the door. I expected him to be lying in the middle of the floor, so imagine how I felt when I looked down and saw the spot I had left him in was empty. I felt like the entire world was closing in on me. I started to panic and wonder how long it had been since he had gotten up from that spot, and did it mean the police were on the way?

I hurried into the room and knelt down, looking under the bed, praying that he had rolled under there, even though I knew the chances of that were slim to none. My heartbeat started racing super-fast.

"Ahhhh!" *Clunk!* I felt something slam into my back. It felt like I had been hit by a school bus. *Clunk!* "You son of a bitch!" I heard Boris holler before he hit me again with whatever he had in his hands.

I fell flat on my stomach and the MAK-90 slid across the carpet. I flipped onto my back to see where the fuck Boris was, but more importantly, what he was hitting me with. I turned over just in time to see this fool with a golf club over his head, ready to bring it down again. "You black son of a bitch! I know Veronica put you up to this!"

Before he could strike me again, I kicked him directly in the nuts. I hurried to a kneeling position and tackled his ass, picking him up and crashing him into the dresser. *Boom!* The big ass mirror fell on top of us and shattered. I slung it off of me, straddled him and proceeded to punch him again and again in the face, feeling my knuckles connect with the bone in his grill. When I punched him in the nose, it broke and got stuck sideways. He hollered and kneed me in the nuts knocking me off of him.

"Get off of me, nigger!" He lunged and dived across the floor, trying to get to the MAK. His hand was almost around the handle.

Even though my nuts were in my stomach, and it felt like I was going to throw up, I bounced up and dived on top of him, right before he could get a firm grasp of the weapon. I bit into the back of his neck.

"Ahhhh! You motherfucker!" he hollered, trying to get away.

I elbowed him in the back of the head once, then punched him as hard as I could on the side of the face. Then, I jumped up and kicked the MAK closer to the door of the room, out of his reach. I hurried and grabbed the golf club and brought it down against his cranium with all of my might. *Whoom!* The driver bussed a hole right through his scope immediately. I took it and brought it down again, aiming for the same spot, because I wanted to see how wide I could get the hole. *Whoom!*

"You bitch-ass, gyro head!" *Whoom! Whoom!* I brought it down repeatedly, until his brains got to spilling out of his head. I got down on my knees and picked up my MAK-90 before jogging out of the room.

I was met by Rip in the hallway. "Look, I got this bitch nigga in the trunk. I gotta have them birds before I kill his ass.

174

You gotta knock Veronica's head off tonight, before she finds out about all of this. I'll meet you back at the spot soon as I'm done with this nigga, Cuz."

I nodded, and ran downstairs and grabbed the pillowcase of money, before hopping into my whip and speeding to the crib. I needed to see my girls and I was missing Lil' Momma like crazy.

It took me thirty minutes to get there. When I got inside of the building, I grabbed the money and ran up the stairs two at a time until I got to our apartment door. I put the key in the lock and pushed it open, stepping in and closing the door behind me. As soon as my eyes adjusted, my heart nearly leaped out of my mouth.

I dropped the bags of money and ran over to Jennifer, wrapping my arms around her. "Jennifer, what's the matter? Where's this blood coming from? And where is Lil' Momma?"

She started crying harder, burying her face into my chest.

To be continued...
Blast For Me 2
Coming Soon

Stay Connected with Us!

Text **LOCKDOWN** to 22828 to stay up-to-date with new releases, sneak peaks, contests and more…

Thank you!

Blast For Me

BOW DOWN TO MY GANGSTA

By **Ca$h & Jamaica**

TORN BETWEEN TWO

By **Coffee**

BLOOD OF A BOSS **IV**

By **Askari**

BRIDE OF A HUSTLA **III**

By **Destiny Skai**

WHEN A GOOD GIRL GOES BAD **II**

By **Adrienne**

LOVE & CHASIN' PAPER **II**

By **Qay Crockett**

THE HEART OF A GANGSTA **II**

By **Jerry Jackson**

LOYAL TO THE GAME **IV**

By **T.J. & Jelissa**

A DOPEBOY'S PRAYER **II**

By **Eddie "Wolf" Lee**

TRUE SAVAGE **III**

By **Chris Green**

IF LOVING YOU IS WRONG… **II**

Ghost

By **Jelissa**

BLOODY COMMAS **III**

By **T.J. Edwards**

BLAST FOR ME **II**

By **Ghost**

A DISTINGUISHED THUG STOLE MY HEART **II**

By **Meesha**

ADDICTIED TO THE DRAMA **II**

By **Jamila Mathis**

Available Now

RESTRAINING ORDER **I & II**

By **CA$H & Coffee**

LOVE KNOWS NO BOUNDARIES **I II & III**

By **Coffee**

RAISED AS A GOON I, II & III

By **Ghost**

LAY IT DOWN **I & II**

LAST OF A DYING BREED

By **Jamaica**

LOYAL TO THE GAME

LOYAL TO THE GAME II

Blast For Me

LOYAL TO THE GAME III

By **TJ & Jelissa**

BLOODY COMMAS

By **T.J. Edwards**

IF LOVING HIM IS WRONG…

By **Jelissa**

A DISTINGUISHED THUG STOLE MY HEART

By **Meesha**

PUSH IT TO THE LIMIT

By **Bre' Hayes**

BLOOD OF A BOSS **I II & III**

By **Askari**

THE STREETS BLEED MURDER **I, II & III**

THE HEART OF A GANGSTA

By **Jerry Jackson**

CUM FOR ME

CUM FOR ME 2

CUM FOR ME 3

An **LDP Erotica Collaboration**

BRIDE OF A HUSTLA **I & II**

THE FETTI GIRLS **I, II& II**

By **Destiny Skai**

WHEN A GOOD GIRL GOES BAD

Ghost

By **Adrienne**

A GANGSTER'S REVENGE **I II III & IV**

THE BOSS MAN'S DAUGHTERS

THE BOSS MAN'S DAUGHTERS II

A SAVAGE LOVE **I & II**

BAE BELONGS TO ME

A HUSTLER'S DECEIT I, II

By **Aryanna**

A KINGPIN'S AMBITON

A KINGPIN'S AMBITION **II**

I MURDER FOR THE DOUGH

By **Ambitious**

TRUE SAVAGE

TRUE SAVAGE II

By **Chris Green**

A DOPEBOY'S PRAYER

By **Eddie "Wolf" Lee**

WHAT ABOUT US **I & II**

NEVER LOVE AGAIN

THUG ADDICTION

By **Kim Kaye**

THE KING CARTEL **I, II & III**

Blast For Me

By **Frank Gresham**

<u>THESE NIGGAS AIN'T LOYAL</u> **I, II & III**

By **Nikki Tee**

<u>GANGSTA SHYT</u> **I II &III**

By **CATO**

<u>THE ULTIMATE BETRAYAL</u>

By **Phoenix**

<u>BOSS'N UP</u> **I & II**

By **Royal Nicole**

<u>I LOVE YOU TO DEATH</u>

By Destiny J

<u>I RIDE FOR MY HITTA</u>

<u>I STILL RIDE FOR MY HITTA</u>

By **Misty Holt**

<u>LOVE & CHASIN' PAPER</u>

By **Qay Crockett**

<u>TO DIE IN VAIN</u>

By **ASAD**

Ghost

BOOKS BY LDP'S CEO, CA$H

TRUST IN NO MAN

TRUST IN NO MAN 2

TRUST IN NO MAN 3

BONDED BY BLOOD

SHORTY GOT A THUG

THUGS CRY

THUGS CRY 2

THUGS CRY 3

TRUST NO BITCH

TRUST NO BITCH 2

TRUST NO BITCH 3

TIL MY CASKET DROPS

RESTRAINING ORDER

RESTRAINING ORDER 2

IN LOVE WITH A CONVICT

Coming Soon

BONDED BY BLOOD 2

BOW DOWN TO MY GANGSTA

Blast For Me

Made in the USA
Coppell, TX
07 December 2021

67373017R00105